The Two Paths

By

John Ruskin, M.A.

The Two Paths
byJohn Ruskin, M.A.

ISBN: 978-93-56569-91-1

Published by

DOUBLE 9 BOOKS

2/13-B, Ansari Road
Daryaganj, New Delhi – 110002
info@double9books.com
www.double9books.com
Tel. 011-40042856

Printed in India.

ABOUT THE AUTHOR

John Ruskin was an English writer, philosopher, art critic, and polymath during the Victorian era. He lived from 8 February 1819 to 20 January 1900. He published on a wide range of topics, including political economy, myth, ornithology, literature, education, and geology. He emphasized the relationships between nature, art, and society in all of his writing.

His father, John James Ruskin (1785-1864) was a wine and sherry importer. At Oxford University and King's College in London, Ruskin studied literature. By studying under Thomas Dale, he prepared for Oxford University (1797-1870).

He fell in love with the Alps at a young age and made his first trip to Venice in 1835. Under the guidance of Charles Runciman, Copley Fielding, and J. D. Harding, he developed his creative abilities.

On April 10, 1848, at her Bowerswell house in Perth, Euphemia "Effie" Gray and John Ruskin were united in marriage. The marriage was troubled, and Effie said that Ruskin was harsh to her. In 1854, six years later, it was revoked.

Ruskin revisited certain topics that had been among his favorites when he was a little kid in the 1880s.

At the age of 80, he passed away from influenza at Brantwood on January 20, 1900. According to his desires, he was buried five days later in the Coniston graveyard.

CONTENTS

PREFACE.

The following addresses, though spoken at different times, are intentionally connected in subject; their aim being to set one or two main principles of art in simple light before the general student, and to indicate their practical bearing on modern design. The law which it has been my effort chiefly to illustrate is the dependence of all noble design, in any kind, on the sculpture or painting of Organic Form.

This is the vital law; lying at the root of all that I have ever tried to teach respecting architecture or any other art. It is also the law most generally disallowed.

I believe this must be so in every subject. We are all of us willing enough to accept dead truths or blunt ones; which can be fitted harmlessly into spare niches, or shrouded and coffined at once out of the way, we holding complacently the cemetery keys, and supposing we have learned something. But a sapling truth, with earth at its root and blossom on its branches; or a trenchant truth, that can cut its way through bars and sods; most men, it seems to me, dislike the sight or entertainment of, if by any means such guest or vision may be avoided. And, indeed, this is no wonder; for one such truth, thoroughly accepted, connects itself strangely with others, and there is no saying what it may lead us to.

And thus the gist of what I have tried to teach about architecture has been throughout denied by my architect readers, even when they thought what I said suggestive in other particulars. "Anything but that. Study Italian Gothic?—perhaps it would be as well: build with pointed arches?—there is no objection: use solid stone and well-burnt brick?— by all means: but—learn to carve or paint organic form ourselves! How can such a thing be asked? We are above all that. The carvers and painters are our servants—quite subordinate people. They ought to be glad if we leave room for them."

Well: on that it all turns. For those who will not learn to carve or paint, and think themselves greater men because they cannot, it is wholly wasted time to read any words of mine; in the truest and sternest sense they can read no words of mine; for the most familiar I can use—"form," "proportion," "beauty," "curvature," "colour"— are used in a sense which by no effort I can communicate to such readers; and in no building that I praise, is the thing that I praise it for, visible to them.

And it is the more necessary for me to state this fully; because so- called Gothic or Romanesque buildings are now rising every day around us, which might be supposed by the public more or less to embody the principles of those styles, but which embody not one of them, nor any shadow or fragment of them; but merely serve to caricature the noble buildings of past ages, and to bring their form into dishonour by leaving out their soul.

The following addresses are therefore arranged, as I have just stated, to put this great law, and one or two collateral ones, in less mistakeable light, securing even in this irregular form at least clearness of assertion. For the rest, the question at issue is not one to be decided by argument, but by experiment, which if the reader is disinclined to make, all demonstration must be useless to him.

The lectures are for the most part printed as they were read, mending only obscure sentences here and there. The parts which were trusted to extempore speaking are supplied, as well as I can remember (only with an addition here and there of things I forgot to say), in the words, or at least the kind of words, used at the time; and they contain, at all events, the substance of what I said more accurately than hurried journal reports. I must beg my readers not in general to trust to such, for even in fast speaking I try to use words carefully; and any alteration of expression will sometimes involve a great alteration in meaning. A little while ago I had to speak of an architectural design, and called it "elegant," meaning, founded on good and well "elected" models; the printed report gave "excellent" design (that is to say, design *excellingly* good), which I did not mean, and should, even in the most hurried speaking, never have said.

The illustrations of the lecture on iron were sketches made too roughly to be engraved, and yet of too elaborate subjects to allow of my drawing them completely. Those now substituted will, however, answer the purpose nearly as well, and are more directly connected with the subjects of the preceding lectures; so that I hope throughout the volume the student will perceive an insistance upon one main truth, nor lose in any minor direction of inquiry the sense of the responsibility which the acceptance of that truth fastens upon him; responsibility for choice, decisive and conclusive, between two modes of study, which involve ultimately the development, or deadening, of every power he possesses. I have tried to hold that choice clearly out to him, and to unveil for him to its farthest the issue of his turning to the right hand or the left. Guides he may find many, and aids many; but all these will be in vain unless he has first recognised the hour and the point of life when the way divides itself, one way leading to the Olive mountains—one to the vale of the Salt Sea. There are few cross roads, that I know of, from one to the other. Let him pause at the parting of THE TWO PATHS.

LECTURE I.

THE DETERIORATIVE POWER OF CONVENTIONAL ART OVER NATIONS.

An Inaugural Lecture, Delivered at the Kensington Museum, January, 1858.

[Footnote: A few introductory words, in which, at the opening of this lecture, I thanked the Chairman (Mr. Cockerell), for his support on the occasion, and asked his pardon for any hasty expressions in my writings, which might have seemed discourteous towards him, or other architects whose general opinions were opposed to mine, may be found by those who care for preambles, not much misreported, in the *Building Chronicle*; with such comments as the genius of that journal was likely to suggest to it.]

As I passed, last summer, for the first time, through the north of Scotland, it seemed to me that there was a peculiar painfulness in its scenery, caused by the non-manifestation of the powers of human art. I had never travelled in, nor even heard or conceived of such a country before; nor, though I had passed much of my life amidst mountain scenery in the south, was I before aware how much of its charm depended on the little gracefulnesses and tendernesses of human work, which are mingled with the beauty of the Alps, or spared by their desolation. It is true that the art which carves and colours the front of a Swiss cottage is not of any very exalted kind; yet it testifies to the completeness and the delicacy of the faculties of the mountaineer; it is true that the remnants of tower and battlement, which afford footing to the wild vine on the Alpine promontory, form but a small part of the great serration of its rocks; and yet it is just that fragment of their broken outline which gives them their pathetic power, and historical majesty. And this element among the wilds of our own country I found wholly wanting. The Highland cottage is literally a heap of gray stones, choked up, rather than roofed over, with black peat and withered heather; the only approach to an effort at decoration consists in the placing of the clods of protective peat obliquely on its roof, so as to give a diagonal arrangement of lines, looking somewhat as if the surface had been scored over by a gigantic claymore.

And, at least among the northern hills of Scotland, elements of more ancient architectural interest are equally absent. The solitary peel- house is hardly discernible by the windings of the stream; the roofless aisle of the priory is lost among the enclosures of the village; and the capital city of the Highlands, Inverness, placed where it might ennoble one of the sweetest landscapes, and by the shore of one of the loveliest estuaries in the world;—placed between the crests of the Grampians and the flowing of the Moray Firth, as if it were a jewel clasping the folds of the mountains to the blue zone of the sea,—is only distinguishable from a distance by one architectural feature, and exalts all the surrounding landscape by no other associations than those which can be connected with its modern castellated gaol.

While these conditions of Scottish scenery affected me very painfully, it being the first time in my life that I had been in any country possessing no valuable monuments or examples of art, they also forced me into the consideration of one or two difficult questions respecting the effect of art on the human mind; and they forced these questions upon me eminently for this reason, that while I was wandering disconsolately among the moors of the Grampians, where there was no art to be found, news of peculiar interest was every day arriving from a country where there was a great deal of art, and art of a delicate kind, to be found. Among the models set before you in this institution, and in the others established throughout the kingdom for the teaching of design, there are, I suppose, none in their kind more admirable than the decorated works of India. They are, indeed, in all materials capable of colour, wool, marble, or metal, almost inimitable in their delicate application of divided hue, and fine arrangement of fantastic line. Nor is this power of theirs exerted by the people rarely, or without enjoyment; the love of subtle design seems universal in the race, and is developed in every implement that they shape, and every building that they raise; it attaches itself with the same intensity, and with the same success, to the service of superstition, of pleasure or of cruelty; and enriches alike, with one profusion on enchanted iridescence, the dome of the pagoda, the fringe of the girdle and the edge of the sword.

So then you have, in these two great populations, Indian and Highland— in the races of the jungle and of the moor—two national capacities distinctly and accurately opposed. On the one side you have a race rejoicing in art, and eminently and universally endowed with the gift of it; on the other you have a people careless of art, and apparently incapable of it, their utmost effort hitherto reaching no farther than to the variation of the positions of the bars of colour in square chequers. And we are thus urged naturally to enquire what is the effect on the moral character, in each nation, of this vast difference in their pursuits and apparent capacities? and whether those rude chequers of the tartan, or the exquisitely fancied involutions of the Cashmere, fold habitually over the noblest hearts? We have had our answer. Since the race of man began its course of sin on this earth, nothing has ever been done by it so significative of all bestial, and lower than bestial degradation, as the acts the Indian race in the year that has just passed by. Cruelty as fierce may indeed have been wreaked, and brutality as abominable been practised before, but never under like circumstances; rage of prolonged war, and resentment of prolonged oppression, have made men as cruel before now; and gradual decline into barbarism, where no examples of decency or civilization existed around them, has sunk, before now, isolated populations to the lowest level of possible humanity. But cruelty stretched to its fiercest against the gentle and unoffending, and corruption festered to its loathsomest in the midst of the witnessing presence of a disciplined civilization,— these we could not have known to be within the practicable compass of human guilt, but for the acts of the Indian mutineer. And, as thus, on the one hand, you have an extreme energy of baseness displayed by these lovers of art; on the other,—as if to put the question into the narrowest compass—you have had an extreme energy of virtue displayed by the despisers of art. Among all the soldiers to whom you owe your victories in the Crimea, and your avenging in the Indies, to none are you bound by closer bonds of gratitude than to the men who have been born and bred among those desolate Highland moors. And thus you have the differences in capacity and circumstance between the two nations, and the differences in result on the moral habits of two nations, put into the most significant—the most palpable—the most brief opposition. Out of the peat cottage come faith, courage, self- sacrifice, purity, and piety, and whatever else is fruitful in the work of Heaven; out of the ivory palace come treachery, cruelty, cowardice, idolatry, bestiality,—whatever else is fruitful in the work of Hell.

But the difficulty does not close here. From one instance, of however great apparent force, it would be wholly unfair to gather any general conclusion—wholly illogical to assert that because we had once found love of art connected with moral baseness, the love of art must be the general root of moral baseness; and equally unfair to assert that, because we had once found neglect of art coincident with nobleness of disposition, neglect of art must be always the source or sign of that nobleness. But if we pass from the Indian peninsula into other countries of the globe; and from our own recent experience, to the records of history, we shall still find one great fact fronting us, in stern universality—namely, the apparent connection of great success in art with subsequent national degradation. You find, in the first place, that the nations which possessed a refined art were always subdued by those who possessed none: you find the Lydian subdued by the Mede; the Athenian by the Spartan; the Greek by the Roman; the Roman by the Goth; the Burgundian by the Switzer: but you find, beyond this—that even where no attack by any external power has accelerated the catastrophe of the state, the period in which any given people reach their highest power in art is precisely that in which they appear to sign the warrant of their own ruin; and that, from the moment in which a perfect statue appears in Florence, a perfect picture in Venice, or a perfect fresco in Rome, from that hour forward, probity, industry, and courage seem to be exiled from their walls, and they perish in a sculpturesque paralysis, or a many-coloured corruption.

But even this is not all. As art seems thus, in its delicate form, to be one of the chief promoters of indolence and sensuality,—so, I need hardly remind you, it hitherto has appeared only in energetic manifestation when it was in the service of superstition. The four greatest manifestations of human intellect which founded the four principal kingdoms of art, Egyptian, Babylonian, Greek, and Italian, were developed by the strong excitement of active superstition in the worship of Osiris, Belus, Minerva, and the Queen of Heaven. Therefore, to speak briefly, it may appear very difficult to show that art has ever yet existed in a consistent and thoroughly energetic school, unless it was engaged in the propagation of falsehood, or the encouragement of vice.

And finally, while art has thus shown itself always active in the service of luxury and idolatry, it has also been strongly directed to the exaltation of cruelty. A nation which lives a pastoral and innocent life never decorates the shepherd's staff or the plough-handle, but races who live by depredation and slaughter nearly always bestow exquisite ornaments on the quiver, the helmet, and the spear.

Does it not seem to you, then, on all these three counts, more than questionable whether we are assembled here in Kensington Museum to any good purpose? Might we not justly be looked upon with suspicion and fear, rather than with sympathy, by the innocent and unartistical public? Are we even sure of ourselves? Do we know what we are about? Are we met here as honest people? or are we not rather so many Catilines assembled to devise the hasty degradation of our country, or, like a conclave of midnight witches, to summon and send forth, on new and unexpected missions, the demons of luxury, cruelty, and superstition?

I trust, upon the whole, that it is not so: I am sure that Mr. Redgrave and Mr. Cole do not at all include results of this kind in their conception of the ultimate objects of the institution which owes so much to their strenuous and well-directed exertions. And I have put this painful question before you, only that we may face it thoroughly, and, as I hope, out-face it. If you will give it a little sincere attention this evening, I trust we may find sufficiently good reasons for our work, and proceed to it hereafter, as all good workmen should do, with clear heads, and calm consciences.

To return, then, to the first point of difficulty, the relations between art and mental disposition in India and Scotland. It is quite true that the art of India is delicate and refined. But it has one curious character distinguishing it from all other art of equal merit in design— *it never represents a natural fact.* It either forms its compositions out of meaningless fragments of colour and flowings of line; or if it represents any living creature, it represents that creature under some distorted and monstrous form. To all the facts and forms of nature it wilfully and resolutely opposes itself; it will not draw a man, but an eight-armed monster; it will not draw a flower, but only a spiral or a zigzag.

It thus indicates that the people who practise it are cut off from all possible sources of healthy knowledge or natural delight; that they have wilfully sealed up and put aside the entire volume of the world, and have got nothing to read, nothing to dwell upon, but that imagination of the thoughts of their hearts, of which we are told that "it is only evil continually." Over the whole spectacle of creation they have thrown a veil in which there is no rent. For them no star peeps through the blanket of the dark—for them neither their heaven shines nor their mountains rise—for them the flowers do not blossom— for them the creatures of field and forest do not live. They lie bound in the dungeon of their own corruption, encompassed only by doleful phantoms, or by spectral vacancy.

Need I remind you what an exact reverse of this condition of mind, as respects the observance of nature, is presented by the people whom we have just been led to contemplate in contrast with the Indian race? You will find upon reflection, that all the highest points of the Scottish character are connected with impressions derived straight from the natural scenery of their country. No nation has ever before shown, in the general tone of its language—in the general current of its literature—so constant a habit of hallowing its passions and confirming its principles by direct association with the charm, or power, of nature. The writings of Scott and Burns—and yet more, of the far greater poets than Burns who gave Scotland her traditional ballads,—furnish you in every stanza—almost in every line—with examples of this association of natural scenery with the passions; [Footnote: The great poets of Scotland, like the great poets of all other countries, never write dissolutely, either in matter or method; but with stern and measured meaning in every syllable. Here's a bit of first-rate work for example:

Tweed said to Till,
'What gars ye rin sae still?'
Till said to Tweed,
'Though ye rin wi' speed,

And I rin slaw,
Whar ye droon ae man,
I droon twa.'"]

but an instance of its farther connection with moral principle struck me forcibly just at the time when I was most lamenting the absence of art among the people. In one of the loneliest districts of Scotland, where the peat cottages are darkest, just at the western foot of that great mass of the Grampians which encircles the sources of the Spey and the Dee, the main road which traverses the chain winds round the foot of a broken rock called Crag, or Craig Ellachie. There is nothing remarkable in either its height or form; it is darkened with a few scattered pines, and touched along its summit with a flush of heather; but it constitutes a kind of headland, or leading promontory, in the group of hills to which it belongs—a sort of initial letter of the mountains; and thus stands in the mind of the inhabitants of the district, the Clan Grant, for a type of their country, and of the influence of that country upon themselves. Their sense of this is beautifully indicated in the war-cry of the clan, "Stand fast, Craig Ellachie." You may think long over those few words without exhausting the deep wells of feeling and thought contained in them—the love of the native land, the assurance of their faithfulness to it; the subdued and gentle assertion of indomitable courage—I *may* need to be told to stand, but, if I do, Craig Ellachie does. You could not but have felt, had you passed beneath it at the time when so many of England's dearest children were being defended by the strength of heart of men born at its foot, how often among the delicate Indian palaces, whose marble was pallid with horror, and whose vermilion was darkened with blood, the remembrance of its rough grey rocks and purple heaths must have risen before the sight of the Highland soldier; how often the hailing of the shot and the shriek of battle would pass away from his hearing, and leave only the whisper of the old pine branches— "Stand fast, Craig Ellachie!"

You have, in these two nations, seen in direct opposition the effects on moral sentiment of art without nature, and of nature without art. And you see enough to justify you in suspecting—while, if you choose to investigate the subject more deeply and with other examples, you will find enough to justify you in *concluding*—that art, followed as such, and for its own sake, irrespective of the interpretation of nature by it, is destructive of whatever is best and noblest in humanity; but that nature, however simply observed, or imperfectly known, is, in the degree of the affection felt for it, protective and helpful to all that is noblest in humanity.

You might then conclude farther, that art, so far as it was devoted to the record or the interpretation of nature, would be helpful and ennobling also.

And you would conclude this with perfect truth. Let me repeat the assertion distinctly and solemnly, as the first that I am permitted to make in this building, devoted in a way so new and so admirable to the service of the art-students of England—Wherever art is practised for its own sake, and the delight of the workman is in what he *does* and *produces*, instead of what he *interprets* or *exhibits*, —there art has an influence of the most fatal kind on brain and heart, and it issues, if long so pursued, in the *destruction both of intellectual power* and *moral principal*; whereas art, devoted humbly and self- forgetfully to the clear statement and record of the facts of the universe, is always helpful and beneficent to mankind, full of comfort, strength, and salvation.

Now, when you were once well assured of this, you might logically infer another thing, namely, that when Art was occupied in the function in which she was serviceable, she would herself be strengthened by the service, and when she was doing what Providence without doubt intended her to do, she would gain in vitality and dignity just as she advanced in usefulness. On the other hand, you might gather, that when her agency was distorted to the deception or degradation of mankind, she would herself be equally misled and degraded—that she would be checked in advance, or precipitated in decline.

And this is the truth also; and holding this clue you will easily and justly interpret the phenomena of history. So long as Art is steady in the contemplation and exhibition of natural facts, so long she herself lives and grows; and in her own life and growth partly implies, partly secures, that of the nation in the midst of which she is practised. But a time has always hitherto come, in which, having thus reached a singular perfection, she begins to contemplate that perfection, and to imitate it, and deduce rules and forms from it; and thus to forget her duty and ministry as the interpreter and discoverer of Truth. And in the very instant when this diversion of her purpose and forgetfulness of her function take place—forgetfulness generally coincident with her apparent perfection—in that instant, I say, begins her actual catastrophe; and by her own fall—so far as she has influence—she accelerates the ruin of the nation by which she is practised.

The study, however, of the effect of art on the mind of nations is one rather for the historian than for us; at all events it is one for the discussion of which we have no more time this evening. But I will ask your patience with me while I try to illustrate, in some further particulars, the dependence of the healthy state and power of art itself upon the exercise of its appointed function in the interpretation of fact.

You observe that I always say *interpretation*, never *imitation*. My reason for so doing is, first, that good art rarely imitates; it usually only describes or explains. But my second and chief reason is that good art always consists of two things: First, the observation of fact; secondly, the manifesting of human design and authority in the way that fact is told. Great and good art must unite the two; it cannot exist for a moment but in their unity; it consists of the two as essentially as water consists of oxygen and hydrogen, or marble of lime and carbonic acid.

Let us inquire a little into the nature of each of the elements. The first element, we say, is the love of Nature, leading to the effort to observe and report her truly. And this is the first and leading element. Review for yourselves the history of art, and you will find this to be a manifest certainty, that *no great school ever yet existed which had not for primal aim the representation of some natural fact as truly as possible*. There have only yet appeared in the world three schools of perfect art—schools, that is to say, that did their work as well as it seems possible to do it. These are the Athenian, [Footnote: See below, the farther notice of the real spirit of Greek work, in the address at Bradford.] Florentine, and Venetian. The Athenian proposed to itself the perfect representation of the form of the human body. It strove to do that as well as it could; it did that as well as it can be done; and all its greatness was founded upon and involved in that single and honest effort. The Florentine school proposed to itself the perfect expression of human emotion— the showing of the effects of passion in the human face and gesture. I call this the Florentine school, because, whether you take Raphael for the culminating master of expressional art in Italy, or Leonardo, or Michael Angelo, you will find that the whole energy of the national effort which produced those masters had its root in Florence; not at Urbino or Milan. I say, then, this Florentine or leading Italian school proposed to itself human expression for its aim in natural truth; it strove to do that as well as it could—did it as well as it can be done—and all its greatness is rooted in that single and honest effort. Thirdly, the Venetian school propose the representation of the effect of colour and shade on all things; chiefly on the human form. It tried to do that as well as it could—did it as well as it can be done—and all its greatness is founded on that single and honest effort.

Pray, do not leave this room without a perfectly clear holding of these three ideas. You may try them, and toss them about afterwards, as much as you like, to see if they'll bear shaking; but do let me put them well and plainly into your possession. Attach them to three works of art which you all have either seen or continually heard of. There's the (so-called) "Theseus" of the Elgin marbles. That represents the whole end and aim of the Athenian school—the natural form of the human body. All their conventional architecture—their graceful shaping and painting of pottery—whatsoever other art they practised—was dependent for its greatness on this sheet-anchor of central aim: true shape of living man. Then take, for your type of the Italian school, Raphael's "Disputa del Sacramento;" that will be an accepted type by everybody, and will involve no possibly questionable points: the Germans will admit it; the English academicians will admit it; and the English purists and pre-Raphaelites will admit it. Well, there you have the truth of human expression proposed as an aim. That is the way people look when they feel this or that—when they have this or that other mental character: are they devotional, thoughtful, affectionate, indignant, or inspired? are they prophets, saints, priests, or kings? then—whatsoever is truly thoughtful, affectionate, prophetic, priestly, kingly—*that* the Florentine school tried to discern, and show; *that* they have discerned and shown; and all their greatness is first fastened in their aim at this central truth—the open expression of the living human soul. Lastly, take Veronese's "Marriage in Cana" in the Louvre. There you have the most perfect representation possible of colour, and light, and shade, as they affect the external aspect of the human form, and its immediate accessories, architecture, furniture, and dress. This external aspect of noblest nature was the first aim of the Venetians, and all their greatness depended on their resolution to achieve, and their patience in achieving it.

Here, then, are the three greatest schools of the former world exemplified for you in three well-known works. The Phidian "Theseus" represents the Greek school pursuing truth of form; the "Disputa" of Raphael, the Florentine school pursuing truth of mental expression; the "Marriage in Cana," the Venetian school pursuing truth of colour and light. But do not suppose that the law which I am stating to you—the great law of art-life—can only be seen in these, the most powerful of all art schools. It is just as manifest in each and every school that ever has had life in it at all. Wheresoever the search after truth begins, there life begins; wheresoever that search ceases, there life ceases. As long as a school of art holds any chain of natural facts, trying to discover more of them and express them better daily, it may play hither and thither as it likes on this side of the chain or that; it may design grotesques and conventionalisms, build the simplest buildings, serve the most practical utilities, yet all it does will be gloriously designed and gloriously done; but let it once quit hold of the chain of natural fact, cease to pursue that as the clue to its work; let it propose to itself any other end than preaching this living word, and think first of showing its own skill or its own fancy, and from that hour its fall is precipitate—its destruction sure; nothing that it does or designs will ever have life or loveliness in it more; its hour has come, and there is no work, nor device, nor knowledge, nor wisdom in the grave whither it goeth.

Let us take for example that school of art over which many of you would perhaps think this law had but little power—the school of Gothic architecture. Many of us may have been in the habit of thinking of that school rather as of one of forms than of facts—a school of pinnacles, and buttresses, and conventional mouldings, and disguise of nature by monstrous imaginings—not a school of truth at all. I think I shall be able, even in the little time we have to-night, to show that this is not so; and that our great law holds just as good at Amiens and Salisbury, as it does at Athens and Florence.

I will go back then first to the very beginnings of Gothic art, and before you, the students of Kensington, as an impanelled jury, I will bring two examples of the barbarism out of which Gothic art emerges, approximately contemporary in date and parallel in executive skill; but, the one, a barbarism that did not get on, and could not get on; the other, a barbarism that could get on, and did get on; and you, the impanelled jury, shall judge what is the essential difference between the two barbarisms, and decide for yourselves what is the seed of life in the one, and the sign of death in the other.

The first,—that which has in it the sign of death,—furnishes us at the same time with an illustration far too interesting to be passed by, of certain principles much depended on by our common modern designers. Taking up one of our architectural publications the other day, and opening it at random, I chanced upon this piece of information, put in rather curious English; but you shall have it as it stands—

"Aristotle asserts, that the greatest species of the beautiful are Order, Symmetry, and the Definite."

I should tell you, however, that this statement is not given as authoritative; it is one example of various Architectural teachings, given in a report in the *Building Chronicle* for May, 1857, of a lecture on Proportion; in which the only thing the lecturer appears to have proved was that,—

The system of dividing the diameter of the shaft of a column into parts for copying the ancient architectural remains of Greece and Rome, adopted by architects from Vitruvius (circa B.C. 25) to the present period, as a method for producing ancient architecture, *is entirely useless,* for the several parts of Grecian architecture cannot be reduced or subdivided by this system; neither does it apply to the architecture of Rome.

Still, as far as I can make it out, the lecture appears to have been one of those of which you will just at present hear so many, the protests of architects who have no knowledge of sculpture—or of any other mode of expressing natural beauty—*against* natural beauty; and their endeavour to substitute mathematical proportions for the knowledge of life they do not possess, and the representation of life of which they are incapable.[Illustration] Now, this substitution of obedience to mathematical law for sympathy with observed life, is the first characteristic of the hopeless work of all ages; as such, you will find it eminently manifested in the specimen I have to give you of the hopeless Gothic barbarism; the barbarism from which nothing could emerge—for which no future was possible but extinction. The Aristotelian principles of the Beautiful are, you remember, Order, Symmetry, and the Definite. Here you have the three, in perfection, applied to the ideal of an angel, in a psalter of the eighth century, existing in the library of St. John's College, Cambridge.[Footnote: I copy this woodcut from Westwood's "Palaeographia Sacra."]

Now, you see the characteristics of this utterly dead school are, first the wilful closing of its eyes to natural facts;—for, however ignorant a person may be, he need only look at a human being to see that it has a mouth as well as eyes; and secondly, the endeavour to adorn or idealize natural fact according to its own notions: it puts red spots in the middle of the hands, and sharpens the thumbs, thinking to improve them. Here you have the most pure type possible of the principles of idealism in all ages: whenever people don't look at Nature, they always think they can improve her. You will also admire, doubtless, the exquisite result of the application of our great modern architectural principle of beauty—symmetry, or equal balance of part by part; you see even the eyes are made symmetrical—entirely round, instead of irregular, oval; and the iris is set properly in the middle, instead of—as nature has absurdly put it—rather under the upper lid. You will also observe the "principle of the pyramid" in the general arrangement of the figure, and the value of "series" in the placing of dots.

From this dead barbarism we pass to living barbarism—to work done by hands quite as rude, if not ruder, and by minds as uninformed; and yet work which in every line of it is prophetic of power, and has in it the sure dawn of day. You have often heard it said that Giotto was the founder of art in Italy. He was not: neither he, nor Giunta Pisano, nor Niccolo Pisano. They all laid strong hands to the work, and brought it first into aspect above ground; but the foundation had been laid for them by the builders of the Lombardic churches in the valleys of the Adda and the Arno. It is in the sculpture of the round arched churches of North Italy, bearing disputable dates, ranging from the eighth to the twelfth century, that you will find the lowest struck roots of the art of Titian and Raphael. [Footnote: I have said elsewhere, "the root of *all* art is struck in the thirteenth century.» This is quite true: but of course some of the smallest fibres run lower, as in this instance.] I go, therefore, to the church which is certainly the earliest of these, St. Ambrogio, of Milan, said still to retain some portions of the actual structure from which St. Ambrose excluded Theodosius, and at all events furnishing the most archaic examples of Lombardic sculpture in North Italy. I do not venture to guess their date; they are barbarous enough for any date.

We find the pulpit of this church covered with interlacing patterns, closely resembling those of the manuscript at Cambridge, but among them is figure sculpture of a very different kind. It is wrought with mere incisions in the stone, of which the effect may be tolerably given by single lines in a drawing. Remember, therefore, for a moment—as characteristic of culminating Italian art—Michael Angelo's fresco of the "Temptation of Eve," in the Sistine chapel, and you will be more interested in seeing the birth of Italian art, illustrated by the same subject, from St. Ambrogio, of Milan, the "Serpent beguiling Eve." [Footnote: This cut is ruder than it should be: the incisions in the marble have a lighter effect than these rough black lines; but it is not worth while to do it better.]

Yet, in that sketch, rude and ludicrous as it is, you have the elements of life in their first form. The people who could do that were sure to get on. For, observe, the workman's whole aim is straight at the facts, as well as he can get them; and not merely at the facts, but at the very heart of the facts. A common workman might have looked at nature for his serpent, but he would have thought only of its scales. But this fellow does not want scales, nor coils; he can do without them; he wants the serpent's heart—malice and insinuation;—and he has actually got them to some extent. So also a common workman, even in this barbarous stage of art, might have carved Eve's arms and body a good deal better; but this man does not care about arms and body, if he can only get at Eve's mind—show that she is pleased at being flattered, and yet in a state of uncomfortable hesitation. And some look of listening, of complacency, and of embarrassment he has verily got:— note the eyes slightly askance, the lips compressed, and the right hand nervously grasping the left arm: nothing can be declared impossible to the people who could begin thus—the world is open to them, and all that is in it; while, on the contrary, nothing is possible to the man who did the symmetrical angel—the world is keyless to him; he has built a cell for himself in which he must abide, barred up for ever— there is no more hope for him than for a sponge or a madrepore.

I shall not trace from this embryo the progress of Gothic art in Italy, because it is much complicated and involved with traditions of other schools, and because most of the students will be less familiar with its results than with their own northern buildings. So, these two designs indicating Death and Life in the beginnings of mediaeval art, we will take an example of the *progress* of that art from our northern work. Now, many of you, doubtless, have been interested by the mass, grandeur, and gloom of Norman architecture, as much as by Gothic traceries; and when you hear me say that the root of all good work lies in natural facts, you doubtless think instantly of your round arches, with their rude cushion capitals, and of the billet or zigzag work by which they are surrounded, and you cannot see what the knowledge of nature has to do with either the simple plan or the rude mouldings. But all those simple conditions of Norman art are merely the expiring of it towards the extreme north. Do not study Norman architecture in Northumberland, but in Normandy, and then you will find that it is just a peculiarly manly, and practically useful, form of the whole great French school of rounded architecture. And where has that French school its origin? Wholly in the rich conditions of sculpture, which, rising first out of imitations of the Roman bas-reliefs, covered all the façades of the French early churches with one continuous arabesque of floral or animal life. If you want to study round-arched buildings, do not go to Durham, but go to Poictiers, and there you will see how all the simple decorations which give you so much pleasure even in their isolated application were invented by persons practised in carving men, monsters, wild animals, birds, and flowers, in overwhelming redundance; and then trace this architecture forward in central France, and you will find it loses nothing of its richness—it only gains in truth, and therefore in grace, until just at the moment of transition into the pointed style, you have the consummate type of the sculpture of the school given you in the west front of the Cathedral of Chartres. From that front I have chosen two fragments to illustrate it. [Footnote: This part of the lecture was illustrated by two drawings, made admirably by Mr. J. T. Laing, with the help of photographs from statues at Chartres. The drawings may be seen at present at the Kensington Museum: but any large photograph of the west front of Chartres will enable the reader to follow what is stated in the lecture, as far as is needful.]

These statues have been long, and justly, considered as representative of the highest skill of the twelfth or earliest part of the thirteenth century in France; and they indeed possess a dignity and delicate charm, which are for the most part wanting in later works. It is owing partly to real nobleness of feature, but chiefly to the grace, mingled with severity, of the falling lines of excessively *thin* drapery; as well as to a most studied finish in composition, every part of the ornamentation tenderly harmonizing with the rest. So far as their power over certain tones of religious mind is owing to a palpable degree of non-naturalism in them, I do not praise it—the exaggerated thinness of body and stiffness of attitude are faults; but they are noble faults, and give the statues a strange look of forming part of the very building itself, and sustaining it—not like the Greek caryatid, without effort—nor like the Renaissance caryatid, by painful or impossible effort—but as if all that was silent and stern, and withdrawn apart, and stiffened in chill of heart against the terror of earth, had passed into a shape of eternal marble; and thus the Ghost had given, to bear up the pillars of the church on earth, all the patient and expectant nature that it needed no more in heaven. This is the transcendental view of the meaning of those sculptures. I do not dwell upon it. What I do lean upon is their purely naturalistic and vital power. They are all portraits—unknown, most of them, I believe, —but palpably and unmistakeably portraits, if not taken from the actual person for whom the statue stands, at all events studied from some living person whose features might fairly represent those of the king or saint intended. Several of them I suppose to be authentic: there is one of a queen, who has evidently, while she lived, been notable for her bright black eyes. The sculptor has cut the iris deep into the stone, and her dark eyes are still suggested with her smile.

There is another thing I wish you to notice specially in these statues —the way in which the floral moulding is associated with the vertical lines of the figure. You have thus the utmost complexity and richness of curvature set side by side with the pure and delicate parallel lines, and both the characters gain in interest and beauty; but there is deeper significance in the thing than that of mere effect in composition; significance not intended on the part of the sculptor, but all the more valuable because unintentional. I mean the close association of the beauty of lower nature in animals and flowers, with the beauty of higher nature in human form. You never get this in Greek work. Greek statues are always isolated; blank fields of stone, or depths of shadow, relieving the form of the statue, as the world of lower nature which they despised retired in darkness from their hearts. Here, the clothed figure seems the type of the Christian spirit—in many respects feebler and more contracted—but purer; clothed in its white robes and crown, and with the riches of all creation at its side.

The next step in the change will be set before you in a moment, merely by comparing this statue from the west front of Chartres with that of the Madonna, from the south transept door of Amiens. [Footnote: There are many photographs of this door and of its central statue. Its sculpture in the tympanum is farther described in the Fourth Lecture.]

This Madonna, with the sculpture round her, represents the culminating power of Gothic art in the thirteenth century. Sculpture has been gaining continually in the interval; gaining, simply because becoming every day more truthful, more tender, and more suggestive. By the way, the old Douglas motto, "Tender and true," may wisely be taken up again by all of us, for our own, in art no less than in other things. Depend upon it, the first universal characteristic of all great art is Tenderness, as the second is Truth. I find this more and more every day: an infinitude of tenderness is the chief gift and inheritance of all the truly great men. It is sure to involve a relative intensity of disdain towards base things, and an appearance of sternness and arrogance in the eyes of all hard, stupid, and vulgar people—quite terrific to such, if they are capable of terror, and hateful to them, if they are capable of nothing higher than hatred. Dante's is the great type of this class of mind. I say the first inheritance is Tenderness— the second Truth, because the Tenderness is in the make of the creature, the Truth in his acquired habits and knowledge; besides, the love comes first in dignity as well as in time, and that is always pure and complete: the truth, at best, imperfect.

To come back to our statue. You will observe that the arrangement of this sculpture is exactly the same as at Chartres—severe falling drapery, set off by rich floral ornament at the side; but the statue is now completely animated: it is no longer fixed as an upright pillar, but bends aside out of its niche, and the floral ornament, instead of being a conventional wreath, is of exquisitely arranged hawthorn. The work, however, as a whole, though perfectly characteristic of the

mean this law to be all that is necessary to form a school. There needs to be much superadded to it, though there never must be anything superseding it. The main thing which needs to be superadded is the gift of design.

It is always dangerous, and liable to diminish the clearness of impression, to go over much ground in the course of one lecture. But I dare not present you with a maimed view of this important subject: I dare not put off to another time, when the same persons would not be again assembled, the statement of the great collateral necessity which, as well as the necessity of truth, governs all noble art.

That collateral necessity is _the visible operation of human intellect in the presentation of truth, _the evidence of what is properly called design or plan in the work, no less than of veracity. A looking-glass does not design—it receives and communicates indiscriminately all that passes before it; a painter designs when he chooses some things, refuses others, and arranges all.

This selection and arrangement must have influence over everything that the art is concerned with, great or small—over lines, over colours, and over ideas. Given a certain group of colours, by adding another colour at the side of them, you will either improve the group and render it more delightful, or injure it, and render it discordant and unintelligible. "Design" is the choosing and placing the colour so as to help and enhance all the other colours it is set beside. So of thoughts: in a good composition, every idea is presented in just that order, and with just that force, which will perfectly connect it with all the other thoughts in the work, and will illustrate the others as well as receive illustration from them; so that the entire chain of thoughts offered to the beholder's mind shall be received by him with as much delight and with as little effort as is possible. And thus you see design, properly so called, is human invention, consulting human capacity. Out of the infinite heap of things around us in the world, it chooses a certain number which it can thoroughly grasp, and presents this group to the spectator in the form best calculated to enable him to grasp it also, and to grasp it with delight.

And accordingly, the capacities of both gatherer and receiver being limited, the object is to make *everything that you offer helpful* and precious. If you give one grain of weight too much, so as to increase fatigue without profit, or bulk without value—that added grain is hurtful; if you put one spot or one syllable out of its proper place, that spot or syllable will be destructive—how far destructive it is almost impossible to tell: a misplaced touch may sometimes annihilate the labour of hours. Nor are any of us prepared to understand the work of any great master, till we feel this, and feel it as distinctly as we do the value of arrangement in the notes of music. Take any noble musical air, and you find, on examining it, that not one even of the faintest or shortest notes can be removed without destruction to the whole passage in which it occurs; and that every note in the passage is twenty times more beautiful so introduced, than it would have been if played singly on the instrument. Precisely this degree of arrangement and relation must exist between every touch [Footnote: Literally. I know how exaggerated this statement sounds; but I mean it,—every syllable of it.—See Appendix IV.] and line in a great picture. You may consider the whole as a prolonged musical composition: its parts, as separate airs connected in the story; its little bits and fragments of colour and line, as separate passages or bars in melodies; and down to the minutest note of the whole—down to the minutest *touch*,—if there is one that can be spared—that one is doing mischief.

Remember therefore always, you have two characters in which all greatness of art consists:—First, the earnest and intense seizing of natural facts; then the ordering those facts by strength of human intellect, so as to make them, for all who look upon them, to the utmost serviceable, memorable, and beautiful. And thus great art is nothing else than the type of strong and noble life; for, as the ignoble person, in his dealings with all that occurs in the world about him, first sees nothing clearly,—looks nothing fairly in the face, and then allows himself to be swept away by the trampling torrent, and unescapable force, of the things that he would not foresee, and could not understand: so the noble person, looking the facts of the world full in the face, and fathoming them with deep faculty, then deals with them in unalarmed intelligence and unhurried strength, and becomes, with his human intellect and will, no unconscious nor insignificant agent, in consummating their good, and restraining their evil.

Thus in human life you have the two fields of rightful toil for ever distinguished, yet for ever associated; Truth first—plan or design, founded thereon; so in art, you have the same two fields for ever distinguished, for ever associated; Truth first—plan, or design, founded thereon.

Now hitherto there is not the least difficulty in the subject; none of you can look for a moment at any great sculptor or painter without seeing the full bearing of these principles. But a difficulty arises when you come to examine the art of a lower order, concerned with furniture and manufacture, for in that art the element of design enters without, apparently, the element of truth. You have often to obtain beauty and display invention without direct representation of nature. Yet, respecting all these things also, the principle is perfectly simple. If the designer of furniture, of cups and vases, of dress patterns, and the like, exercises himself continually in the imitation of natural form in some leading division of his work; then, holding by this stem of life, he may pass down into all kinds of merely geometrical or formal design with perfect safety, and with noble results.[Footnote: This principle, here cursorily stated, is one of the chief subjects of inquiry in the following Lectures.] Thus Giotto, being primarily a figure painter and sculptor, is, secondarily, the richest of all designers in mere mosaic of coloured bars and triangles; thus Benvenuto Cellini, being in all the higher branches of metal work a perfect imitator of nature, is in all its lower branches the best designer of curve for lips of cups and handles of vases; thus Holbein, exercised primarily in the noble art of truthful portraiture, becomes, secondarily, the most exquisite designer of embroideries of robe, and blazonries on wall; and thus Michael Angelo, exercised primarily in the drawing of body and limb, distributes in the mightiest masses the order of his pillars, and in the loftiest shadow the hollows of his dome. But once quit hold of this living stem, and set yourself to the designing of ornamentation, either in the ignorant play of your own heartless fancy, as the Indian does, or according to received application of heartless laws, as the modern European does, and there is but one word for you—Death:— death of every healthy faculty, and of every noble intelligence, incapacity of understanding one great work that man has ever done, or of doing anything that it shall be helpful for him to behold. You have cut yourselves off voluntarily, presumptuously, insolently, from the whole teaching of your Maker in His Universe; you have cut yourselves off from it, not because you were forced to mechanical labour for your bread—not because your fate had appointed you to wear away your life in walled chambers, or dig your life out of dusty furrows; but, when your whole profession, your whole occupation— all the necessities and chances of your existence, led you straight to the feet of the great Teacher, and thrust you into the treasury of His works; where you have nothing to do but to live by gazing, and to grow by wondering;—wilfully you bind up your eyes from the splendour—wilfully bind up your life-blood from its beating—wilfully turn your backs upon all the majesties of Omnipotence—wilfully snatch your hands from all the aids of love, and what can remain for you, but helplessness and blindness,—except the worse fate than the being blind yourselves—that of becoming Leaders of the blind?

Do not think that I am speaking under excited feeling, or in any exaggerated terms. I have written the words I use, that I may know what I say, and that you, if you choose, may see what I have said. For, indeed, I have set before you tonight, to the best of my power, the sum and substance of the system of art to the promulgation of which I have devoted my life hitherto, and intend to devote what of life may still be spared to me. I have had but one steady aim in all that I have ever tried to teach, namely—to declare that whatever was great in human art was the expression of man's delight in God's work.

And at this time I have endeavoured to prove to you—if you investigate the subject you may more entirely prove to yourselves—that no school ever advanced far which had not the love of natural fact as a primal energy. But it is still more important for you to be assured that the conditions of life and death in the art of nations are also the conditions of life and death in your own; and that you have it, each in his power at this very instant, to determine in which direction his steps are turning. It seems almost a terrible thing to tell you, that all here have all the power of knowing at once what hope there is for them as artists; you would, perhaps, like better that there was some unremovable doubt about the chances of the future—some possibility that you might be advancing, in unconscious ways, towards unexpected successes—some excuse or reason for going about, as students do so often, to this master or the other, asking him if they have genius, and whether they are doing right, and gathering, from his careless or formal replies, vague flashes of encouragement, or fitfulnesses of despair. There is no need for this—no excuse for it. All of you have the trial of yourselves in your own power; each may undergo at this instant, before his own judgment seat, the ordeal by fire. Ask yourselves what is the leading motive which actuates you while you are at work. I do not ask you what your leading motive is for working—that is a different thing; you may have families to support—parents to help—brides to win; you may have all these, or other such sacred and pre-eminent motives, to press the morning's labour and prompt the twilight thought. But when you are fairly *at* the work, what is the motive then which tells upon every touch of it? If it is the love of that which your work represents—if, being a landscape painter, it is love of hills and trees that moves you—if, being a figure painter, it is love of human beauty and human soul that moves you— if, being a flower or animal painter, it is love, and wonder, and delight in petal and in limb that move you, then the Spirit is upon you, and the earth is yours, and the fulness thereof. But if, on the other hand, it is petty self-complacency in your own skill, trust in precepts and laws, hope for academical or popular approbation, or avarice of wealth,—it is quite possible that by steady industry, or even by fortunate chance, you may win the applause, the position, the fortune, that you desire;— but one touch of true art you will never lay on canvas or on stone as long as you live.

Make, then, your choice, boldly and consciously, for one way or other it *must* be made. On the dark and dangerous side are set, the pride which delights in self-contemplation—the indolence which rests in unquestioned forms—the ignorance that despises what is fairest among God›s creatures, and the dulness that denies what is marvellous in His working: there is a life of monotony for your own souls, and of misguiding for those of others. And, on the other side, is open to your choice the life of the crowned spirit, moving as a light in creation— discovering always—illuminating always, gaining every hour in strength, yet bowed down every hour into deeper humility; sure of being right in its aim, sure of being irresistible in its progress; happy in what it has securely done—happier in what, day by day, it may as securely hope; happiest at the close of life, when the right hand begins to forget its cunning, to remember, that there never was a touch of the chisel or the pencil it wielded, but has added to the knowledge and quickened the happiness of mankind.

LECTURE II.

THE UNITY OF ART.

Part of an Address delivered at Manchester, 14th March, 1859.

[Footnote: I was prevented, by press of other engagements, from preparing this address with the care I wished; and forced to trust to such expression as I could give at the moment to the points of principal importance; reading, however, the close of the preceding lecture, which I thought contained some truths that would bear repetition. The whole was reported, better than it deserved, by Mr. Pitman, of the *Manchester Courier*, and published nearly verbatim. I have here extracted, from the published report, the facts which I wish especially to enforce; and have a little cleared their expression; its loose and colloquial character I cannot now help, unless by re-writing the whole, which it seems not worth while to do.]

It is sometimes my pleasant duty to visit other cities, in the hope of being able to encourage their art students; but here it is my pleasanter privilege to come for encouragement myself. I do not know when I have received so much as from the report read this evening by Mr. Hammersley, bearing upon a subject which has caused me great anxiety. For I have always felt in my own pursuit of art, and in my endeavors to urge the pursuit of art on others, that while there are many advantages now that never existed before, there are certain grievous difficulties existing, just in the very cause that is giving the stimulus to art—in the immense spread of the manufactures of every country which is now attending vigorously to art. We find that manufacture and art are now going on always together; that where there is no manufacture there is no art. I know how much there is of pretended art where there is no manufacture: there is much in Italy, for instance; no country makes so bold pretence to the production of new art as Italy at this moment; yet no country produces so little.

If you glance over the map of Europe, you will find that where the manufactures are strongest, there art also is strongest. And yet I always felt that there was an immense difficulty to be encountered by the students who were in these centres of modern movement. They had to avoid the notion that art and manufacture were in any respect one. Art may be healthily associated with manufacture, and probably in future will always be so; but the student must be strenuously warned against supposing that they can ever be one and the same thing, that art can ever be followed on the principles of manufacture. Each must be followed separately; the one must influence the other, but each must be kept distinctly separate from the other.

It would be well if all students would keep clearly in their mind the real distinction between those words which we use so often, "Manufacture," "Art," and "Fine Art." "MANUFACTURE" is, according to the etymology and right use of the word, "the making of anything by hands,"—directly or indirectly, with or without the help of instruments or machines. Anything proceeding from the hand of man is manufacture; but it must have proceeded from his hand only, acting mechanically, and uninfluenced at the moment by direct intelligence.

Then, secondly, ART is the operation of the hand and the intelligence of man together; there is an art of making machinery; there is an art of building ships; an art of making carriages; and so on. All these, properly called Arts, but not Fine Arts, are pursuits in which the hand of man and his head go together, working at the same instant.

Then FINE ART is that in which the hand, the head, and the *heart* of man go together.

Recollect this triple group; it will help you to solve many difficult problems. And remember that though the hand must be at the bottom of everything, it must also go to the top of everything; for Fine Art must be produced by the hand of man in a much greater and clearer sense than manufacture is. Fine Art must always be produced by the subtlest of all machines, which is the human hand. No machine yet contrived, or hereafter contrivable, will ever equal the fine machinery of the human fingers. Thoroughly perfect art is that which proceeds from the heart, which involves all the noble emotions;—associates with these the head, yet as inferior to the heart; and the hand, yet as inferior to the heart and head; and thus brings out the whole man.

Hence it follows that since Manufacture is simply the operation of the hand of man in producing that which is useful to him, it essentially separates itself from the emotions; when emotions interfere with machinery they spoil it: machinery must go evenly, without emotion. But the Fine Arts cannot go evenly; they always must have emotion ruling their mechanism, and until the pupil begins to feel, and until all he does associates itself with the current of his feeling, he is not an artist. But pupils in all the schools in this country are now exposed to all kinds of temptations which blunt their feelings. I constantly feel discouraged in addressing them because I know not how to tell them boldly what they ought to do, when I feel how practically difficult it is for them to do it. There are all sorts of demands made upon them in every direction, and money is to be made in every conceivable way but the right way. If you paint as you ought, and study as you ought, depend upon it the public will take no notice of you for a long while. If you study wrongly, and try to draw the attention of the public upon you,—supposing you to be clever students—you will get swift reward; but the reward does not come fast when it is sought wisely; it is always held aloof for a little while; the right roads of early life are very quiet ones, hedged in from nearly all help or praise. But the wrong roads are noisy,—vociferous everywhere with all kinds of demand upon you for art which is not properly art at all; and in the various meetings of modern interests, money is to be made in every way; but art is to be followed only in *one* way. That is what I want mainly to say to you, or if not to you yourselves (for, from what I have heard from your excellent master to-night, I know you are going on all rightly), you must let me say it through you to others. Our Schools of Art are confused by the various teaching and various interests that are now abroad among us. Everybody is talking about art, and writing about it, and more or less interested in it; everybody wants art, and there is not art for everybody, and few who talk know what they are talking about; thus students are led in all variable ways, while there is only one way in which they can make steady progress, for true art is always and will be always one. Whatever changes may be made in the customs of society, whatever new machines we may invent, whatever new manufactures we may supply, Fine Art must remain what it was two thousand years ago, in the days of Phidias; two thousand years hence, it will be, in all its principles, and in all its great effects upon the mind of man, just the same. Observe this that I say, please, carefully, for I mean it to the very utmost. *There is but one right way of doing any given thing required of an artist*; there may be a hundred wrong, deficient, or mannered ways, but there is only one complete and right way. Whenever two artists are trying to do the same thing with the same materials, and do it in different ways, one of them is wrong; he may be charmingly wrong, or impressively wrong—various circumstances in his temper may make his wrong pleasanter than any person's right; it may for him, under his given limitations of knowledge or temper, be better perhaps that he should err in his own way than try for anybody else's—but for all that his way is wrong, and it is essential for all masters of schools to know what the right way is, and what right art is, and to see how simple and how single all right art has been, since the beginning of it.

But farther, not only is there but one way of *doing* things rightly, but there is only one way of *seeing* them, and that is, seeing the whole of them, without any choice, or more intense perception of one point than another, owing to our special idiosyncrasies. Thus, when Titian or Tintoret look at a human being, they see at a glance the whole of its nature, outside and in; all that it has of form, of colour, of passion, or of thought; saintliness, and loveliness; fleshly body, and spiritual power; grace, or strength, or softness, or whatsoever other quality, those men will see to the full, and so paint, that, when narrower people come to look at what they have done, every one may, if he chooses, find his own special pleasure in the work. The sensualist will find sensuality in Titian; the thinker will find thought; the saint, sanctity; the colourist, colour; the anatomist, form; and yet the picture will never be a popular one in the full sense, for none of these narrower people will find their special taste so alone consulted, as that the qualities which would ensure their gratification shall be sifted or separated from others; they are checked by the presence of the other qualities which ensure the gratification of other men. Thus, Titian is not soft enough for the sensualist, Correggio suits him better; Titian is not defined enough for the formalist,—Leonardo suits him better; Titian is not pure enough for the religionist,—Raphael suits him better; Titian is not polite enough for the man of the world,—Vandyke suits him better; Titian is not forcible enough for the lovers of the picturesque,— Rembrandt suits him better. So Correggio is popular with a certain set, and Vandyke with a certain set, and Rembrandt with a certain set. All are great men, but of inferior stamp, and therefore Vandyke is popular, and Rembrandt is popular, [Footnote: And Murillo, of all true painters the narrowest, feeblest, and most superficial, for those reasons the most popular.] but nobody cares much at heart about Titian; only there is a strange under-current of everlasting murmur about his name, which means the deep consent of all great men that he is greater than they— the consent of those who, having sat long enough at his feet, have found in that restrained harmony of his strength there are indeed depths of each balanced power more wonderful than all those separate manifestations in inferior painters: that there is a softness more exquisite than Correggio's, a purity loftier than Leonardo's, a force mightier than Rembrandt's, a sanctity more solemn even than Raffaelle's.

Do not suppose that in saying this of Titian, I am returning to the old eclectic theories of Bologna; for all those eclectic theories, observe, were based, not upon an endeavour to unite the various characters of nature (which it is possible to do), but the various narrownesses of taste, which it is impossible to do. Rubens is not more vigorous than Titian, but less vigorous; but because he is so narrow-minded as to enjoy vigour only, he refuses to give the other qualities of nature, which would interfere with that vigour and with our perception of it. Again, Rembrandt is not a greater master of chiaroscuro than Titian;— he is a less master, but because he is so narrow-minded as to enjoy chiaroscuro only, he withdraws from you the splendour of hue which would interfere with this, and gives you only the shadow in which you can at once feel it.

Now all these specialties have their own charm in their own way: and there are times when the particular humour of each man is refreshing to us from its very distinctness; but the effort to add any other qualities to this refreshing one instantly takes away the distinctiveness, and therefore the exact character to be enjoyed in its appeal to a particular humour in us. Our enjoyment arose from a weakness meeting a weakness, from a partiality in the painter fitting to a partiality in us, and giving us sugar when we wanted sugar, and myrrh when we wanted myrrh; but sugar and myrrh are not meat: and when we want meat and bread, we must go to better men.

The eclectic schools endeavoured to unite these opposite partialities and weaknesses. They trained themselves under masters of exaggeration, and tried to unite opposite exaggerations. That was impossible. They did not see that the only possible eclecticism had been already accomplished;—the eclecticism of temperance, which, by the restraint of force, gains higher force; and by the self-denial of delight, gains higher delight. This you will find is ultimately the case with every true and right master; at first, while we are tyros in art, or before we have earnestly studied the man in question, we shall see little in him; or perhaps see, as we think, deficiencies; we shall fancy he is inferior to this man in that, and to the other man in the other; but as we go on studying him we shall find that he has got both that and the other; and both in a far higher sense than the man who seemed to possess those qualities in excess. Thus in Turner's lifetime, when people first looked at him, those who liked rainy, weather, said he was not equal to Copley Fielding; but those who looked at Turner long enough found that he could be much more wet than Copley Fielding, when he chose. The people who liked force, said that "Turner was not strong enough for them; he was effeminate; they liked De Wint,—nice strong tone;—or Cox—great, greeny, dark masses of colour—solemn feeling of the freshness and depth of nature;—they liked Cox—Turner was too hot for them." Had they looked long enough they would have found that he had far more force than De Wint, far more freshness than Cox when he chose,—only united with other elements; and that he didn't choose to be cool, if nature had appointed the weather to be hot. The people who liked Prout said "Turner had not firmness of hand—he did not know enough about architecture—he was not picturesque enough." Had they looked at his architecture long, they would have found that it contained subtle picturesquenesses, infinitely more picturesque than anything of Prout's. People who liked Callcott said that "Turner was not correct or pure enough—had no classical taste." Had they looked at Turner long enough they would have found him as severe, when he chose, as the greater Poussin;— Callcott, a mere vulgar imitator of other men's high breeding. And so throughout with all thoroughly great men, their strength is not seen at first, precisely because they unite, in due place and measure, every great quality.

Now the question is, whether, as students, we are to study only these mightiest men, who unite all greatness, or whether we are to study the works of inferior men, who present us with the greatness which we particularly like? That question often comes before me when I see a strong idiosyncrasy in a student, and he asks me what he should study. Shall I send him to a true master, who does not present the quality in a prominent way in which that student delights, or send him to a man with whom he has direct sympathy? It is a hard question. For very curious results have sometimes been brought out, especially in late years, not only by students following their own bent, but by their being withdrawn from teaching altogether. I have just named a very great man in his own field—Prout. We all know his drawings, and love them: they have a peculiar character which no other architectural drawings ever possessed, and which no others can possess, because all Prout's subjects are being knocked down or restored. (Prout did not like restored buildings any more than I do.) There will never be any more Prout drawings. Nor could he have been what he was, or expressed with that mysteriously effective touch that peculiar delight in broken and old buildings, unless he had been withdrawn from all high art influence. You know that Prout was born of poor parents— that he was educated down in Cornwall;—and that, for many years, all the art- teaching he had was his own, or the fishermen's. Under the keels of the fishing-boats, on the sands of our southern coasts, Prout learned all that he needed to learn about art. Entirely by himself, he felt his way to this particular style, and became the painter of pictures which I think we should all regret to lose. It becomes a very difficult question what that man would have been, had he been brought under some entirely wholesome artistic influence, He had immense gifts of composition. I do not know any man who had more power of invention than Prout, or who had a sublimer instinct in his treatment of things; but being entirely withdrawn from all artistical help, he blunders his way to that short-coming representation, which, by the very reason of its short-coming, has a certain charm we should all be sorry to lose. And therefore I feel embarrassed when a student comes to me, in whom I see a strong instinct of that kind: and cannot tell whether I ought to say to him, "Give up all your studies of old boats, and keep away from the sea-shore, and come up to the Royal Academy in London, and look at nothing but Titian." It is a difficult thing to make up one's mind to say that. However, I believe, on the whole, we may wisely leave such matters in the hands of Providence; that if we have the power of teaching the right to anybody, we should teach them the right; if we have the power of showing them the best thing, we should show them the best thing; there will always, I fear, be enough want of teaching, and enough bad teaching, to bring out very curious erratical results if we want them. So, if we are to teach at all, let us teach the right thing, and ever the right thing. There are many attractive qualities inconsistent with rightness;—do not let us teach them,—let us be content to waive them. There are attractive qualities in Burns, and attractive qualities in Dickens, which neither of those writers would have possessed if the one had been educated, and the other had been studying higher nature than that of cockney London; but those attractive qualities are not such as we should seek in a school of literature. If we want to teach young men a good manner of writing, we should teach it from Shakspeare,—not from Burns; from Walter Scott,— and not from Dickens. And I believe that our schools of painting are at present inefficient in their action, because they have not fixed on this high principle what are the painters to whom to point; nor boldly resolved to point to the best, if determinable. It is becoming a matter of stern necessity that they should give a simple direction to the attention of the student, and that they should say, "This is the mark you are to aim at; and you are not to go about to the print-shops, and peep in, to see how this engraver does that, and the other engraver does the other, and how a nice bit of character has been caught by a new man, and why this odd picture has caught the popular attention. You are to have nothing to do with all that; you are not to mind about popular attention just now; but here is a thing which is eternally right and good: you are to look at that, and see if you cannot do something eternally right and good too."

But suppose you accept this principle: and resolve to look to some great man, Titian, or Turner, or whomsoever it may be, as the model of perfection in art;—then the question is, since this great man pursued his art in Venice, or in the fields of England, under totally different conditions from those possible to us now—how are you to make your study of him effective here in Manchester? how bring it down into patterns, and all that you are called upon as operatives to produce? how make it the means of your livelihood, and associate inferior branches of art with this great art? That may become a serious doubt to you. You may think there is some other way of producing clever, and pretty, and saleable patterns than going to look at Titian, or any other great man. And that brings me to the question, perhaps the most vexed question of all amongst us just now, between conventional and perfect art. You know that among architects and artists there are, and have been almost always, since art became a subject of much discussion, two parties, one maintaining that nature should be always altered and modified, and that the artist is greater than nature; they do not maintain, indeed, in words, but they maintain in idea, that the artist is greater than the Divine Maker of these things, and can improve them; while the other party say that he cannot improve nature, and that nature on the whole should improve him. That is the real meaning of the two parties, the essence of them; the practical result of their several theories being that the Idealists are always producing more or less formal conditions of art, and the Realists striving to produce in all their art either some image of nature, or record of nature; these, observe, being quite different things, the image being a resemblance, and the record, something which will give information about nature, but not necessarily imitate it.

[Footnote: The portion of the lecture here omitted was a recapitulation of that part of the previous one which opposed conventional art to natural art.]

* * * * *

You may separate these two groups of artists more distinctly in your mind as those who seek for the pleasure of art, in the relations of its colours and lines, without caring to convey any truth with it; and those who seek for the truth first, and then go down from the truth to the pleasure of colour and line. Marking those two bodies distinctly as separate, and thinking over them, you may come to some rather notable conclusions respecting the mental dispositions which are involved in each mode of study. You will find that large masses of the art of the world fall definitely under one or the other of these heads. Observe, pleasure first and truth afterwards, (or not at all,) as with the Arabians and Indians; or, truth first and pleasure afterwards, as with Angelico and all other great European painters. You will find that the art whose end is pleasure only is pre-eminently the gift of cruel and savage nations, cruel in temper, savage in habits and conception; but that the art which is especially dedicated to natural fact always indicates a peculiar gentleness and tenderness of mind, and that all great and successful work of that kind will assuredly be the production of thoughtful, sensitive, earnest, kind men, large in their views of life, and full of various intellectual power. And farther, when you examine the men in whom the gifts of art are variously mingled, or universally mingled, you will discern that the ornamental, or pleasurable power, though it may be possessed by good men, is not in itself an indication of their goodness, but is rather, unless balanced by other faculties, indicative of violence of temper, inclining to cruelty and to irreligion. On the other hand, so sure as you find any man endowed with a keen and separate faculty of representing natural fact, so surely you will find that man gentle and upright, full of nobleness and breadth of thought. I will give you two instances, the first peculiarly English, and another peculiarly interesting because it occurs among a nation not generally very kind or gentle.

I am inclined to think that, considering all the disadvantages of circumstances and education under which his genius was developed, there was perhaps hardly ever born a man with a more intense and innate gift of insight into nature than our own Sir Joshua Reynolds. Considered as a painter of individuality in the human form and mind, I think him, even as it is, the prince of portrait painters. Titian paints nobler pictures, and Vandyke had nobler subjects, but neither of them entered so subtly as Sir Joshua did into the minor varieties of human heart and temper; arid when you consider that, with a frightful conventionality of social habitude all around him, he yet conceived the simplest types of all feminine and childish loveliness;—that in a northern climate, and with gray, and white, and black, as the principal colours around him, he yet became a colourist who can be crushed by none, even of the Venetians;—and that with Dutch painting and Dresden china for the prevailing types of art in the saloons of his day, he threw himself at once at the feet of the great masters of Italy, and arose from their feet to share their throne—I know not that in the whole history of art you can produce another instance of so strong, so unaided, so unerring an instinct for all that was true, pure, and noble.

Now, do you recollect the evidence respecting the character of this man,—the two points of bright peculiar evidence given by the sayings of the two greatest literary men of his day, Johnson and Goldsmith? Johnson, who, as you know, was always Reynolds' attached friend, had but one complaint to make against him, that he hated nobody:—"Reynolds," he said, "you hate no one living; I like a good hater!" Still more significant is the little touch in Goldsmith's "Retaliation." You recollect how in that poem he describes the various persons who met at one of their dinners at St. James's Coffee-house, each person being described under the name of some appropriate dish. You will often hear the concluding lines about Reynolds Quoted—

"He shifted his trumpet," &c;—

less often, or at least less attentively, the preceding ones, far more important—

«Still born to improve us in every part—
His pencil our faces, his *manners our heart;*"

and never, the most characteristic touch
of all, near the beginning:—

«Our dean shall be venison, just fresh from the plains;
Our Burke shall be tongue, with a garnish of brains.
To make out the dinner, full certain I am,
That Rich is anchovy, and Reynolds is *lamb*."

The other painter whom I would give you as an instance of this gentleness is a man of another nation, on the whole I suppose one of the most cruel civilized nations in the world—the Spaniards. They produced but one great painter, only one; but he among the very greatest of painters, Velasquez. You would not suppose, from looking at Velasquez' portraits generally, that he was an especially kind or good man; you perceive a peculiar sternness about them; for they were as true as steel, and the persons whom he had to paint being not generally kind or good people, they were stern in expression, and Velasquez gave the sternness; but he had precisely the same intense perception of truth, the same marvellous instinct for the rendering of all natural soul and all natural form that our Reynolds had. Let me, then, read you his character as it is given by Mr. Stirling, of Kier:—

"Certain charges, of what nature we are not informed, brought against him after his death, made it necessary for his executor, Fuensalida, to refute them at a private audience granted to him by the king for that purpose. After listening to the defence of his friend, Philip immediately made answer: 'I can believe all you say of the excellent disposition of Diego Velasquez.' Having lived for half his life in courts, he was yet capable both of gratitude and generosity, and in the misfortunes, he could remember the early kindness of

Olivares. The friend of the exile of Loeches, it is just to believe that he was also the friend of the all-powerful favourite at Buenretiro. No mean jealousy ever influenced his conduct to his brother artists; he could afford not only to acknowledge the merits, but to forgive the malice, of his rivals. His character was of that *rare and happy kind, in which high intellectual power is combined with indomitable strength of will, and a winning sweetness of temper,* and which seldom fails to raise the possessor above his fellow-men, making his life a

'laurelled victory, and smooth success Be strewed before his feet.'"

I am sometimes accused of trying to make art too moral; yet, observe, I do not say in the least that in order to be a good painter you must be a good man; but I do say that in order to be a good natural painter there must be strong elements of good in the mind, however warped by other parts of the character. There are hundreds of other gifts of painting which are not at all involved with moral conditions, but this one, the perception of nature, is never given but under certain moral conditions. Therefore, now you have it in your choice; here are your two paths for you: it is required of you to produce conventional ornament, and you may approach the task as the Hindoo does, and as the Arab did, —without nature at all, with the chance of approximating your disposition somewhat to that of the Hindoos and Arabs; or as Sir Joshua and Velasquez did, with, not the chance, but the certainty, of approximating your disposition, according to the sincerity of your effort—to the disposition of those great and good men.

And do you suppose you will lose anything by approaching your conventional art from this higher side? Not so. I called, with deliberate measurement of my expression, long ago, the decoration of the Alhambra "detestable," not merely because indicative of base conditions of moral being, but because merely as decorative work, however captivating in some respects, it is wholly wanting in the real, deep, and intense qualities of ornamental art. Noble conventional decoration belongs only to three periods. First, there is the conventional decoration of the Greeks, used in subordination to their sculpture. There are then the noble conventional decoration of the early Gothic schools, and the noble conventional arabesque of the great Italian schools. All these were reached from above, all reached by stooping from a knowledge of the human form. Depend upon it you will find, as you look more and more into the matter, that good subordinate ornament has ever been rooted in a higher knowledge; and if you are again to produce anything that is noble, you must have the higher knowledge first, and descend to all lower service; condescend as much as you like,—condescension never does any man any harm,—but get your noble standing first. So, then, without any scruple, whatever branch of art you may be inclined as a student here to follow,—whatever you are to make your bread by, I say, so far as you have time and power, make yourself first a noble and accomplished artist; understand at least what noble and accomplished art is, and then you will be able to apply your knowledge to all service whatsoever.

I am now going to ask your permission to name the masters whom I think it would be well if we could agree, in our Schools of Art in England, to consider our leaders. The first and chief I will not myself presume to name; he shall be distinguished for you by the authority of those two great painters of whom we have just been speaking—Reynolds and Velasquez. You may remember that in your Manchester Art Treasures Exhibition the most impressive things were the works of those two men— nothing told upon the eye so much; no other pictures retained it with such a persistent power. Now, I have the testimony, first of Reynolds to Velasquez, and then of Velasquez to the man whom I want you to take as the master of all your English schools. The testimony of Reynolds to Velasquez is very striking. I take it from some fragments which have just been published by Mr. William Cotton—precious fragments—of Reynolds' diaries, which I chanced upon luckily as I was coming down here: for I was going to take Velasquez' testimony alone, and then fell upon this testimony of Reynolds to Velasquez, written most fortunately in Reynolds' own hand-you may see the manuscript. "What *we* are all,» said Reynolds, «attempting to do with great labor, Velasquez does at once." Just think what is implied when a man of the enormous power and facility that Reynolds had, says he was "trying to do with great labor" what Velasquez "did at once."

Having thus Reynolds' testimony to Velasquez, I will take Velasquez' testimony to somebody else. You know that Velasquez was sent by Philip of Spain to Italy, to buy pictures for him. He went all over Italy, saw the living artists there, and all their best pictures when freshly painted, so that he had every opportunity of judging;

and never was a man so capable of judging. He went to Rome and ordered various works of living artists; and while there, he was one day asked by Salvator Rosa what he thought of Raphael. His reply, and the ensuing conversation, are thus reported by Boschini, in curious Italian verse, which, thus translated by Dr. Donaldson, is quoted in Mr. Stirling's Life of Velasquez:—

> «The master» [Velasquez] «stiffly bowed his figure tall
> And said, 'For Rafael, to speak the truth—
> I always was plain-spoken from my youth—
> I cannot say I like his works at all.'

> «›Well,› said the other» [Salvator], ‹if you can run down
> So great a man, I really cannot see
> What you can find to like in Italy;
> To him we all agree to give the crown.'

> «Diego answered thus: ‹I saw in Venice
> The true test of the good and beautiful;
> First in my judgment, ever stands that school,
> And Titian first of all Italian men is.›»

"Tizian ze quel die porta la bandiera"

Learn that line by heart and act, at all events for some time to come, upon Velasquez' opinion in that matter. Titian is much the safest master for you. Raphael's power, such as it characters in his mind; it is "Raphaelesque," properly so called; but Titian's power is simply the power of doing right. Whatever came before Titian, he did wholly as it *ought* to be done. Do not suppose that now in recommending Titian to you so strongly, and speaking of nobody else to-night, I am retreating in anywise from what some of you may perhaps recollect in my works, the enthusiasm with which I have always spoken of another Venetian painter. There are three Venetians who are never separated in my mind—Titian, Veronese, and Tintoret. They all have their own unequalled gifts, and Tintoret especially has imagination and depth of soul which I think renders him indisputably the greatest man; but, equally indisputably, Titian is the greatest painter; and therefore the greatest painter who ever lived. You may be led wrong by Tintoret [Footnote: See Appendix I.—"Right and Wrong."] in many respects, wrong by Raphael in more; all that you learn from Titian will be right. Then, with Titian, take Leonardo, Rembrandt, and

Albert Dürer. I name those three masters for this reason: Leonardo has powers of subtle drawing which are peculiarly applicable in many ways to the drawing of fine ornament, and are very useful for all students. Rembrandt and Dürer are the only men whose actual work of hand you can have to look at; you can have Rembrandt's etchings, or Dürer's engravings actually hung in your schools; and it is a main point for the student to see the real thing, and avoid judging of masters at second-hand. As, however, in obeying this principle, you cannot often have opportunities of studying Venetian painting, it is desirable that you should have a useful standard of colour, and I think it is possible for you to obtain this. I cannot, indeed, without entering upon ground which might involve the hurting the feelings of living artists, state exactly what I believe to be the relative position of various painters in England at present with respect to power of colour. But I may say this, that in the peculiar gifts of colour which will be useful to you as students, there are only one or two of the pre-Raphaelites, and William Hunt, of the old Water Colour Society, who would be safe guides for you: and as quite a safe guide, there is nobody but William Hunt, because the pre-Raphaelites are all more or less affected by enthusiasm and by various morbid conditions of intellect and temper; but old William Hunt—I am sorry to say "old," but I say it in a loving way, for every year that has added to his life has added also to his skill—William Hunt is as right as the Venetians, as far as he goes, and what is more, nearly as inimitable as they. And I think if we manage to put in the principal schools of England a little bit of Hunt's work, and make that somewhat of a standard of colour, that we can apply his principles of colouring to subjects of all kinds. Until you have had a work of his long near you; nay, unless you have been labouring at it, and trying to copy it, you do not know the thoroughly grand qualities that are concentrated in it. Simplicity, and intensity, both of the highest character;— simplicity of aim, and intensity of power and success, are involved in that man's unpretending labour.

Finally, you cannot believe that I would omit my own favourite, Turner. I fear from the very number of his works left to the nation, that there is a disposition now rising to look upon his vast bequest with some contempt. I beg of you, if in nothing else, to believe me in this, that you cannot further the art of England in any way more distinctly than by giving attention to every fragment that has been left by that man. The time will come when his full power and right place will be acknowledged; that time will not be for many a day yet: nevertheless, be assured—as far as you are inclined to give the least faith to anything I may say to you, be assured—that you can act for the good of art in England in no better way than by using whatever influence any of you have in any direction to urge the reverent study and yet more reverent preservation of the works of Turner. I do not say "the exhibition" of his works, for we are not altogether ripe for it: they are still too far above us; uniting, as I was telling you, too many qualities for us yet to feel fully their range and their influence;— but let us only try to keep them safe from harm, and show thoroughly and conveniently what we show of them at all, and day by day their greatness will dawn upon us more and more, and be the root of a school of art in England, which I do not doubt may be as bright, as just, and as refined as even that of Venice herself. The dominion of the sea seems to have been associated, in past time, with dominion in the arts also: Athens had them together; Venice had them together; but by so much as our authority over the ocean is wider than theirs over the Ćgean or Adriatic, let us strive to make our art more widely beneficent than theirs, though it cannot be more exalted; so working out the fulfilment, in their wakening as well as their warning sense, of those great words of the aged Tintoret:

"Sempre si fa il mare maggiore."

LECTURE III.

MODERN MANUFACTURE AND DESIGN.

A Lecture delivered at Bradford, March, 1859.

It is with a deep sense of necessity for your indulgence that I venture to address you to-night, or that I venture at any time to address the pupils of schools of design intended for the advancement of taste in special branches of manufacture. No person is able to give useful and definite help towards such special applications of art, unless he is entirely familiar with the conditions of labour and natures of material involved in the work; and indefinite help is little better than no help at all. Nay, the few remarks which I propose to lay before you this evening will, I fear, be rather suggestive of difficulties than helpful in conquering them: nevertheless, it may not be altogether unserviceable to define clearly for you (and this, at least, I am able to do) one or two of the more stern general obstacles which stand at present in the way of our success in design; and to warn you against exertion of effort in any vain or wasteful way, till these main obstacles are removed.

The first of these is our not understanding the scope and dignity of Decorative design. With all our talk about it, the very meaning of the words "Decorative art" remains confused and undecided. I want, if possible, to settle this question for you to-night, and to show you that the principles on which you must work are likely to be false, in proportion as they are narrow; true, only as they are founded on a perception of the connection of all branches of art with each other.

Observe, then, first—the only essential distinction between Decorative and other art is the being fitted for a fixed place; and in that place, related, either in subordination or command, to the effect of other pieces of art. And all the greatest art which the world has produced is thus fitted for a place, and subordinated to a purpose. There is no existing highest-order art but is decorative. The best sculpture yet produced has been the decoration of a temple front—the best painting, the decoration of a room. Raphael's best doing is merely the wall- colouring of a suite of apartments in the Vatican, and his cartoons were made for tapestries. Correggio's best doing is the decoration of two small church cupolas at Parma; Michael Angelo's of a ceiling in the Pope's private chapel; Tintoret's, of a ceiling and side wall belonging to a charitable society at Venice; while Titian and Veronese threw out their noblest thoughts, not even on the inside, but on the outside of the common brick and plaster walls of Venice.

Get rid, then, at once of any idea of Decorative art being a degraded or a separate kind of art. Its nature or essence is simply its being fitted for a definite place; and, in that place, forming part of a great and harmonious whole, in companionship with other art; and so far from this being a degradation to it—so far from Decorative art being inferior to other art because it is fixed to a spot—on the whole it may be considered as rather a piece of degradation that it should be portable. Portable art—independent of all place—is for the most part ignoble art. Your little Dutch landscape, which you put over your sideboard to-day, and between the windows tomorrow, is a far more contemptible piece of work than the extents of field and forest with which Benozzo has made green and beautiful the once melancholy arcade of the Campo Santo at Pisa; and the wild boar of silver which you use for a seal, or lock into a velvet case, is little likely to be so noble a beast as the bronze boar who foams forth the fountain from under his tusks in the market-place of Florence. It is, indeed, possible that the portable picture or image may be first-rate of its kind, but it is not first-rate because it is portable; nor are Titian's frescoes less than first-rate because they are fixed; nay, very frequently the highest compliment you can pay to a cabinet picture is to say—"It is as grand as a fresco."

Keeping, then, this fact fixed in our minds,—that all art *may* be decorative, and that the greatest art yet produced has been decorative,—we may proceed to distinguish the orders and dignities of decorative art, thus:—

I. The first order of it is that which is meant for places where it cannot be disturbed or injured, and where it can be perfectly seen; and then the main parts of it should be, and have always been made, by the great masters, as perfect, and as full of nature as possible.

You will every day hear it absurdly said that room decoration should be by flat patterns—by dead colours—by conventional monotonies, and I know not what. Now, just be assured of this—nobody ever yet used conventional art to decorate with, when he could do anything better, and knew that what he did would be safe. Nay, a great painter will always give you the natural art, safe or not. Correggio gets a commission to paint a room on the ground floor of a palace at Parma: any of our people—bred on our fine modern principles—would have covered it with a diaper, or with stripes or flourishes, or mosaic patterns. Not so Correggio: he paints a thick trellis of vine-leaves, with oval openings, and lovely children leaping through them into the room; and lovely children, depend upon it, are rather more desirable decorations than diaper, if you can do them—but they are not quite so easily done. In like manner Tintoret has to paint the whole end of the Council Hall at Venice. An orthodox decorator would have set himself to make the wall look like a wall—Tintoret thinks it would be rather better, if he can manage it, to make it look a little like Paradise;— stretches his canvas right over the wall, and his clouds right over his canvas; brings the light through his clouds—all blue and clear—zodiac beyond zodiac; rolls away the vaporous flood from under the feet of saints, leaving them at last in infinitudes of light—unorthodox in the last degree, but, on the whole, pleasant.

And so in all other cases whatever, the greatest decorative art is wholly unconventional—downright, pure, good painting and sculpture, but always fitted for its place; and subordinated to the purpose it has to serve in that place.

II. But if art is to be placed where it is liable to injury—to wear and tear; or to alteration of its form; as, for instance, on domestic utensils, and armour, and weapons, and dress; in which either the ornament will be worn out by the usage of the thing, or will be cast into altered shape by the play of its folds; then it is wrong to put beautiful and perfect art to such uses, and you want forms of inferior art, such as will be by their simplicity less liable to injury; or, by reason of their complexity and continuousness, may show to advantage, however distorted by the folds they are cast into.

And thus arise the various forms of inferior decorative art, respecting which the general law is, that the lower the place and office of the thing, the less of natural or perfect form you should have in it; a zigzag or a chequer is thus a better, because a more consistent ornament for a cup or platter than a landscape or portrait is: hence the general definition of the true forms of conventional ornament is, that they consist in the bestowal of as much beauty on the object as shall be consistent with its Material, its Place, and its Office.

Let us consider these three modes of consistency a little.

(A.) Conventionalism by cause of inefficiency of material.

If, for instance, we are required to represent a human figure with stone only, we cannot represent its colour; we reduce its colour to whiteness. That is not elevating the human body, but degrading it; only it would be a much greater degradation to give its colour falsely. Diminish beauty as much as you will, but do not misrepresent it. So again, when we are sculpturing a face, we can't carve its eyelashes. The face is none the better for wanting its eyelashes—it is injured by the want; but would be much more injured by a clumsy representation of them.

Neither can we carve the hair. We must be content with the conventionalism of vile solid knots and lumps of marble, instead of the golden cloud that encompasses the fair human face with its waving mystery. The lumps of marble are not an elevated representation of hair—they are a degraded one; yet better than any attempt to imitate hair with the incapable material.

In all cases in which such imitation is attempted, instant degradation to a still lower level is the result. For the effort to imitate shows that the workman has only a base and poor conception of the beauty of the reality—else he would know his task to be hopeless, and give it up at once; so that all endeavours to avoid conventionalism, when the material demands it, result from insensibility to truth, and are among the worst forms of vulgarity. Hence, in the greatest Greek statues, the hair is very slightly indicated—not because the sculptor disdained hair, but because he knew what it was too well to touch it insolently. I do not doubt but that the Greek painters drew hair exactly as Titian does. Modern attempts to produce finished pictures on glass result from the same base vulgarism. No man who knows what painting means, can endure a painted glass window which emulates painter's work. But he rejoices in a glowing mosaic of broken colour:

for that is what the glass has the special gift and right of producing. [Footnote: See Appendix II., Sir Joshua Reynolds's disappointment.]

(B.) Conventionalism by cause of inferiority of place.

When work is to be seen at a great distance, or in dark places, or in some other imperfect way, it constantly becomes necessary to treat it coarsely or severely, in order to make it effective. The statues on cathedral fronts, in good times of design, are variously treated according to their distances: no fine execution is put into the features of the Madonna who rules the group of figures above the south transept of Rouen at 150 feet above the ground; but in base modern work, as Milan Cathedral, the sculpture is finished without any reference to distance; and the merit of every statue is supposed to consist in the visitor's being obliged to ascend three hundred steps before he can see it.

(C.) Conventionalism by cause of inferiority of office.

When one piece of ornament is to be subordinated to another (as the moulding is to the sculpture it encloses, or the fringe of a drapery to the statue it veils), this inferior ornament needs to be degraded in order to mark its lower office; and this is best done by refusing, more or less, the introduction of natural form. The less of nature it contains, the more degraded is the ornament, and the fitter for a humble place; but, however far a great workman may go in refusing the higher organisms of nature, he always takes care to retain the magnificence of natural lines; that is to say, of the infinite curves, such as I have analyzed in the fourth volume of "Modern Painters." His copyists, fancying that they can follow him without nature, miss precisely the essence of all the work; so that even the simplest piece of Greek conventional ornament loses the whole of its value in any modern imitation of it, the finer curves being always missed. Perhaps one of the dullest and least justifiable mistakes which have yet been made about my writing, is the supposition that I have attacked or despised Greek work. I have attacked Palladian work, and modern imitation of Greek work. Of Greek work itself I have never spoken but with a reverence quite infinite: I name Phidias always in exactly the same tone with which I speak of Michael Angelo, Titian, and Dante. My first statement of this faith, now thirteen years ago, was surely clear enough. "We shall see by this light three colossal images standing up side by side, looming in their great rest of spirituality above the whole world horizon. Phidias, Michael Angelo, and Dante,—from these we may go down step by step among the mighty men of every age, securely and certainly observant of diminished lustre in every appearance of restlessness and effort, until the last trace of inspiration vanishes in the tottering affectation or tortured insanities of modern times." ("Modern Painters," vol. ii., p. 253.) This was surely plain speaking enough, and from that day to this my effort has been not less continually to make the heart of Greek work known than the heart of Gothic: namely, the nobleness of conception of form derived from perpetual study of the figure; and my complaint of the modern architect has been not that he followed the Greeks, but that he denied the first laws of life in theirs as in all other art.

The fact is, that all good subordinate forms of ornamentation ever yet existent in the world have been invented, and others as beautiful can only be invented, by men primarily exercised in drawing or carving the human figure. I will not repeat here what I have already twice insisted upon, to the students of London and Manchester, respecting the degradation of temper and intellect which follows the pursuit of art without reference to natural form, as among the Asiatics: here, I will only trespass on your patience so far as to mark the inseparable connection between figure-drawing and good ornamental work, in the great European schools, and all that are connected with them.

Tell me, then, first of all, what ornamental work is usually put before our students as the type of decorative perfection? Raphael's arabesques; are they not? Well, Raphael knew a little about the figure, I suppose, before he drew them. I do not say that I like those arabesques; but there are certain qualities in them which are inimitable by modern designers; and those qualities are just the fruit of the master's figure study. What is given the student as next to Raphael's work? Cinquecento ornament generally. Well, cinquecento generally, with its birds, and cherubs, and wreathed foliage, and clustered fruit, was the amusement of men who habitually and easily carved the figure, or painted it. All the truly fine specimens of it have figures or animals as main parts of the design.

"Nay, but," some anciently or mediévally minded person will exclaim, "we don't want to study cinquecento. We want severer, purer conventionalism." What will you have? Egyptian ornament? Why, the whole mass of it is made up of multitudinous human figures in every kind of action—and magnificent action; their kings drawing their bows in their chariots, their sheaves of arrows rattling at their shoulders; the slain falling under them as before a pestilence; their captors driven before them in astonied troops; and do you expect to imitate Egyptian ornament without knowing how to draw the human figure? Nay, but you will take Christian ornament—purest mediaeval Christian—thirteenth century! Yes: and do you suppose you will find the Christian less human? The least natural and most purely conventional ornament of the Gothic schools is that of their painted glass; and do you suppose painted glass, in the fine times, was ever wrought without figures? We have got into the way, among our other modern wretchednesses, of trying to make windows of leaf diapers, and of strips of twisted red and yellow bands, looking like the patterns of currant jelly on the top of Christmas cakes; but every casement of old glass contained a saint's history. The windows of Bourges, Chartres, or Rouen have ten, fifteen, or twenty medallions in each, and each medallion contains two figures at least, often six or seven, representing every event of interest in the history of the saint whose life is in question. Nay, but, you say those figures are rude and quaint, and ought not to be imitated. Why, so is the leafage rude and quaint, yet you imitate that. The coloured border pattern of geranium or ivy leaf is not one whit better drawn, or more like geraniums and ivy, than the figures are like figures; but you call the geranium leaf idealized—why don't you call the figures so? The fact is, neither are idealized, but both are conventionalized on the same principles, and in the same way; and if you want to learn how to treat the leafage, the only way is to learn first how to treat the figure. And you may soon test your powers in this respect. Those old workmen were not afraid of the most familiar subjects. The windows of Chartres were presented by the trades of the town, and at the bottom of each window is a representation of the proceedings of the tradesmen at the business which enabled them to pay for the window. There are smiths at the forge, curriers at their hides, tanners looking into their pits, mercers selling goods over the counter—all made into beautiful medallions. Therefore, whenever you want to know whether you have got any real power of composition or adaptation in ornament, don't be content with sticking leaves together by the ends,—anybody can do that; but try to conventionalize a butcher's or a greengrocer's, with Saturday night customers buying cabbage and beef. That will tell you if you can design or not.

I can fancy your losing patience with me altogether just now. "We asked this fellow down to tell our workmen how to make shawls, and he is only trying to teach them how to caricature." But have a little patience with me, and examine, after I have done, a little for yourselves into the history of ornamental art, and you will discover why I do this. You will discover, I repeat, that all great ornamental art whatever is founded on the effort of the workman to draw the figure, and, in the best schools, to draw all that he saw about him in living nature. The best art of pottery is acknowledged to be that of Greece, and all the power of design exhibited in it, down to the merest zigzag, arises primarily from the workman having been forced to outline nymphs and knights; from those helmed and draped figures he holds his power. Of Egyptian ornament I have just spoken. You have everything given there that the workman saw; people of his nation employed in hunting, fighting, fishing, visiting, making love, building, cooking—everything they did is drawn, magnificently or familiarly, as was needed. In Byzantine ornament, saints, or animals which are types of various spiritual power, are the main subjects; and from the church down to the piece of enamelled metal, figure,— figure,—figure, always principal. In Norman and Gothic work you have, with all their quiet saints, also other much disquieted persons, hunting, feasting, fighting, and so on; or whole hordes of animals racing after each other. In the Bayeux tapestry, Queen Matilda gave, as well as she could,—in many respects graphically enough,—the whole history of the conquest of England. Thence, as you increase in power of art, you have more and more finished figures, up to the solemn sculptures of Wells Cathedral, or the cherubic enrichments of the Venetian Madonna dei Miracoli. Therefore, I will tell you fearlessly, for I know it is true, you must raise your workman up to life, or you will never get from him one line of well-imagined conventionalism. We have at present no good ornamental design. We can't have it yet, and we must be patient if we want to have it. Do not hope to feel the effect of your schools at once, but raise the men as high as you can, and then let them stoop as low as you need; no great man ever minds stooping. Encourage the students, in sketching accurately and continually from nature anything that comes in their way—still life, flowers, animals; but, above all, figures; and so far as you allow of any difference between an artist's training and theirs, let it be, not in what they draw, but in the degree of conventionalism you require in the sketch.

For my own part, I should always endeavour to give thorough artistical training first; but I am not certain (the experiment being yet untried) what results may be obtained by a truly intelligent practice of conventional drawing, such as that of the Egyptians, Greeks, or thirteenth century French, which consists in the utmost possible rendering of natural form by the fewest possible lines. The animal and bird drawing of the Egyptians is, in their fine age, quite magnificent under its conditions; magnificent in two ways—first, in keenest perception of the main forms and facts in the creature; and, secondly, in the grandeur of line by which their forms are abstracted and insisted on, making every asp, ibis, and vulture a sublime spectre of asp or ibis or vulture power. The way for students to get some of this gift again (some only, for I believe the fulness of the gift itself to be connected with vital superstition, and with resulting intensity of reverence; people were likely to know something about hawks and ibises, when to kill one was to be irrevocably judged to death) is never to pass a day without drawing some animal from the life, allowing themselves the fewest possible lines and colours to do it with, but resolving that whatever is characteristic of the animal shall in some way or other be shown. [Footnote: Plate 75 in Vol. V. of Wilkinson's "Ancient Egypt" will give the student an idea of how to set to work.] I repeat, it cannot yet be judged what results might be obtained by a nobly practised conventionalism of this kind; but, however that may be, the first fact,—the necessity of animal and figure drawing, is absolutely certain, and no person who shrinks from it will ever become a great designer.

One great good arises even from the first step in figure drawing, that it gets the student quit at once of the notion of formal symmetry. If you learn only to draw a leaf well, you are taught in some of our schools to turn it the other way, opposite to itself; and the two leaves set opposite ways are called "a design:" and thus it is supposed possible to produce ornamentation, though you have no more brains than a looking-glass or a kaleidoscope has. But if you once learn to draw the human figure, you will find that knocking two men's heads together does not necessarily constitute a good design; nay, that it makes a very bad design, or no design at all; and you will see at once that to arrange a group of two or more figures, you must, though perhaps it may be desirable to balance, or oppose them, at the same time vary their attitudes, and make one, not the reverse of the other, but the companion of the other.

I had a somewhat amusing discussion on this subject with a friend, only the other day; and one of his retorts upon me was so neatly put, and expresses so completely all that can either be said or shown on the opposite side, that it is well worth while giving it you exactly in the form it was sent to me. My friend had been maintaining that the essence of ornament consisted in three things:—contrast, series, and symmetry. I replied (by letter) that "none of them, nor all of them together, would produce ornament. Here"—(making a ragged blot with the back of my pen on the paper)—"you have contrast; but it isn't ornament: here, 1, 2, 3, 4, 5, 6,"—(writing the numerals)—"You have series; but it isn't ornament: and here,"—(sketching a rough but symmetrical "stick- figure" sketch of a human body at the side)—"you have symmetry; but it isn't ornament."

My friend replied:—

"Your materials were not ornament, because you did not apply them. I send them to you back, made up into a choice sporting neckerchief:"

[Illustration: Sketch of a square of cloth decorated with a diagonal grid pattern of stick-figure human forms, with repeated and reflected ink-blot shapes at the corners and the digits 1 through 6 arranged into simple symmetrical shapes and repeated around the border.]

Symmetrical figure Unit of diaper.
Contrast Corner ornaments.
Series Border ornaments.

"Each figure is converted into a harmony by being revolved on its two axes, the whole opposed in contrasting series."

My answer was—or rather was to the effect (for I must expand it a little, here)—that his words, "because you did not apply them," contained the gist of the whole matter;—that the application of them, or any other things, was precisely the essence of design; the non-application, or wrong application, the negation of design: that his use of the poor materials was in this case admirable; and that if he could explain to me, in clear words, the principles on which he had so used them, he would be doing a very great service to all students of art.

"Tell me, therefore (I asked), these main points:

"1. How did you determine the number of figures you would put into the neckerchief? Had there been more, it would have been mean and ineffective,—a pepper-and-salt sprinkling of figures. Had there been fewer, it would have been monstrous. How did you fix the number?

"2. How did you determine the breadth of the border and relative size of the numerals?

"3. Why are there two lines outside of the border, and one only inside? Why are there no more lines? Why not three and two, or three and five? Why lines at all to separate the barbarous figures; and why, if lines at all, not double or treble instead of single?

"4. Why did you put the double blots at the corners? Why not at the angles of the chequers,—or in the middle of the border?

"It is precisely your knowing why *not* to do these things, and why to do just what you have done, which constituted your power of design; and like all the people I have ever known who had that power, you are entirely unconscious of the essential laws by which you work, and confuse other people by telling them that the design depends on symmetry and series, when, in fact, it depends entirely on your own sense and judgment."

This was the substance of my last answer—to which (as I knew beforehand would be the case) I got no reply; but it still remains to be observed that with all the skill and taste (especially involving the architect's great trust, harmony of proportion), which my friend could bring to bear on the materials given him, the result is still only—a sporting neckerchief—that is to say, the materials addressed, first, to recklessness, in the shape of a mere blot; then to computativeness in a series of figures; and then to absurdity and ignorance, in the shape of an ill-drawn caricature—such materials, however treated, can only work up into what will please reckless, computative, and vulgar persons,— that is to say, into a sporting neckerchief. The difference between this piece of ornamentation and Correggio's painting at Parma lies simply and wholly in the additions (somewhat large ones), of truth and of tenderness: in the drawing being lovely as well as symmetrical— and representative of realities as well as agreeably disposed. And truth, tenderness, and inventive application or disposition are indeed the roots of ornament—not contrast, nor symmetry.

It ought yet farther to be observed, that *the nobler the materials, the less their symmetry is endurable.* In the present case, the sense of fitness and order, produced by the repetition of the figures, neutralizes, in some degree, their reckless vulgarity; and is wholly, therefore, beneficent to them. But draw the figures better, and their repetition will become painful. You may harmlessly balance a mere geometrical form, and oppose one quatrefoil or cusp by another exactly like it. But put two Apollo Belvideres back to back, and you will not think the symmetry improves them. *Whenever the materials of ornament are noble, they must be various*; and repetition of parts is either the sign of utterly bad, hopeless, and base work; or of the intended degradation of the parts in which such repetition is allowed, in order to foil others more noble.

Such, then, are a few of the great principles, by the enforcement of which you may hope to promote the success of the modern student of design; but remember, none of these principles will be useful at all, unless you understand them to be, in one profound and stern sense, useless. [Footnote: I shall endeavour for the future to put my self-contradictions in short sentences and direct terms, in order to save sagacious persons the trouble of looking for them.]

That is to say, unless you feel that neither you nor I, nor any one, can, in the great ultimate sense, teach anybody how to make a good design.

If designing *could* be taught, all the world would learn: as all the world reads—or calculates. But designing is not to be spelled, nor summed. My men continually come to me, in my drawing class in London, thinking I am to teach them what is instantly to enable them to gain their bread. "Please, sir, show us how to design." "Make designers of us." And you, I doubt not, partly expect me to tell you to-night how to make designers of your Bradford youths. Alas! I could as soon tell you how to make or manufacture an ear of wheat, as to make a good artist of any kind. I can analyze the wheat very learnedly for you—tell you there is starch in it, and carbon, and silex. I can give you starch, and charcoal, and flint; but you are as far from your ear of wheat as you were before. All that can possibly be done for any one who wants ears of wheat is to show them where to find grains of wheat, and how to sow them, and then, with patience, in Heaven's time, the ears will come—or will perhaps come—ground and weather permitting. So in this matter of making artists—first you must find your artist in the grain; then you must plant him; fence and weed the field about him; and with patience, ground and weather permitting, you may get an artist out of him—not otherwise. And what I have to speak to you about, tonight, is mainly the ground and the weather, it being the first and quite most material question in this matter, whether the ground and weather of Bradford, or the ground and weather of England in general,—suit wheat.

And observe in the outset, it is not so much what the present circumstances of England are, as what we wish to make them, that we have to consider. If you will tell me what you ultimately intend Bradford to be, perhaps I can tell you what Bradford can ultimately produce. But you must have your minds clearly made up, and be distinct in telling me what you do want. At present I don't know what you are aiming at, and possibly on consideration you may feel some doubt whether you know yourselves. As matters stand, all over England, as soon as one mill is at work, occupying two hundred hands, we try, by means of it, to set another mill at work, occupying four hundred. That is all simple and comprehensive enough—but what is it to come to? How many mills do we want? or do we indeed want no end of mills? Let us entirely understand each other on this point before we go any farther. Last week, I drove from Rochdale to Bolton Abbey; quietly, in order to see the country, and certainly it was well worth while. I never went over a more interesting twenty miles than those between Rochdale and Burnley. Naturally, the valley has been one of the most beautiful in the Lancashire hills; one of the far away solitudes, full of old shepherd ways of life. At this time there are not,—I speak deliberately, and I believe quite literally,—there are not, I think, more than a thousand yards of road to be traversed anywhere, without passing a furnace or mill.

Now, is that the kind of thing you want to come to everywhere? Because, if it be, and you tell me so distinctly, I think I can make several suggestions to-night, and could make more if you give me time, which would materially advance your object. The extent of our operations at present is more or less limited by the extent of coal and ironstone, but we have not yet learned to make proper use of our clay. Over the greater part of England, south of the manufacturing districts, there are magnificent beds of various kinds of useful clay; and I believe that it would not be difficult to point out modes of employing it which might enable us to turn nearly the whole of the south of England into a brickfield, as we have already turned nearly the whole of the north into a coal-pit. I say "nearly" the whole, because, as you are doubtless aware, there are considerable districts in the south composed of chalk renowned up to the present time for their downs and mutton. But, I think, by examining carefully into the conceivable uses of chalk, we might discover a quite feasible probability of turning all the chalk districts into a limekiln, as we turn the clay districts into a brickfield. There would then remain nothing but the mountain districts to be dealt with; but, as we have not yet ascertained all the uses of clay and chalk, still less have we ascertained those of stone; and I think, by draining the useless inlets of the Cumberland, Welsh, and Scotch lakes, and turning them, with their rivers, into navigable reservoirs and canals, there would be no difficulty in working the whole of our mountain districts as a gigantic quarry of slate and granite, from which all the rest of the world might be supplied with roofing and building stone.

Is this, then, what you want? You are going straight at it at present; and I have only to ask under what limitations I am to conceive or describe your final success? Or shall there be no limitations? There are none to your powers; every day puts new machinery at your disposal, and increases, with your capital, the vastness of your undertakings. The changes in the state of this country are now so rapid, that it would be wholly absurd to endeavour to lay down laws of art education for it under its present aspect and circumstances; and therefore I must necessarily ask, how much of it do you seriously intend within the next fifty years to be coal-pit, brickfield, or quarry? For the sake of distinctness of conclusion, I will suppose your success absolute: that from shore to shore the whole of the island is to be set as thick with chimneys as the masts stand in the docks of Liverpool: and there shall be no meadows in it; no trees; no gardens; only a little corn grown upon the housetops, reaped and threshed by steam: that you do not leave even room for roads, but travel either over the roofs of your mills, on viaducts; or under their floors, in tunnels: that, the smoke having rendered the light of the sun unserviceable, you work always by the light of your own gas: that no acre of English ground shall be without its shaft and its engine; and therefore, no spot of English ground left, on which it shall be possible to stand, without a definite and calculable chance of being blown off it, at any moment, into small pieces.

Under these circumstances, (if this is to be the future of England,) no designing or any other development of beautiful art will be possible. Do not vex your minds, nor waste your money with any thought or effort in the matter. Beautiful art can only be produced by people who have beautiful things about them, and leisure to look at them; and unless you provide some elements of beauty for your workmen to be surrounded by, you will find that no elements of beauty can be invented by them.

I was struck forcibly by the bearing of this great fact upon our modern efforts at ornamentation in an afternoon walk, last week, in the suburbs of one of our large manufacturing towns. I was thinking of the difference in the effect upon the designer's mind, between the scene which I then came upon, and the scene which would have presented itself to the eyes of any designer of the middle ages, when he left his workshop. Just outside the town I came upon an old English cottage, or mansion, I hardly know which to call it, set close under the hill, and beside the river, perhaps built somewhere in the Charles's time, with mullioned windows and a low arched porch; round which, in the little triangular garden, one can imagine the family as they used to sit in old summer times, the ripple of the river heard faintly through the sweetbrier hedge, and the sheep on the far-off wolds shining in the evening sunlight. There, uninhabited for many and many a year, it had been left in unregarded havoc of ruin; the garden-gate still swung loose to its latch; the garden, blighted utterly into a field of ashes, not even a weed taking root there; the roof torn into shapeless rents; the shutters hanging about the windows in rags of rotten wood; before its gate, the stream which had gladdened it now soaking slowly by, black as ebony, and thick with curdling scum; the bank above it trodden into unctuous, sooty slime: far in front of it, between it and the old hills, the furnaces of the city foaming forth perpetual plague of sulphurous darkness; the volumes of their storm clouds coiling low over a waste of grassless fields, fenced from each other, not by hedges, but by slabs of square stone, like gravestones, riveted together with iron.

That was your scene for the designer's contemplation in his afternoon walk at Rochdale. Now fancy what was the scene which presented itself, in his afternoon walk, to a designer of the Gothic school of Pisa—Nino Pisano, or any of his men.

On each side of a bright river he saw rise a line of brighter palaces, arched and pillared, and inlaid with deep red porphyry, and with serpentine; along the quays before their gates were riding troops of knights, noble in face and form, dazzling in crest and shield; horse and man one labyrinth of quaint colour and gleaming light—the purple, and silver, and scarlet fringes flowing over the strong limbs and clashing mail, like sea-waves over rocks at sunset. Opening on each side from the river were gardens, courts, and cloisters; long successions of white pillars among wreaths of vine; leaping of fountains through buds of pomegranate and orange: and still along the garden-paths, and under and through the crimson of the pomegranate shadows, moving slowly, groups of the fairest women that Italy ever saw—fairest, because purest and thoughtfullest; trained in all high knowledge, as in all courteous art—in dance, in song, in sweet wit, in lofty learning, in loftier courage, in loftiest love—able alike to cheer, to enchant, or save, the souls of men. Above all this scenery of perfect human life, rose dome and bell-tower, burning with white alabaster and gold; beyond dome and bell-tower the slopes of mighty hills, hoary with olive; far in the north, above a purple sea of peaks of solemn Apennine, the clear, sharp-cloven Carrara mountains sent up their steadfast flames of marble summit into amber sky; the great sea itself, scorching with expanse of light, stretching from their feet to the Gorgonian isles; and over all these, ever present, near or far— seen through the leaves of vine, or imaged with all its march of clouds in the Arno's stream, or set with its depth of blue close against the golden hair and burning cheek of lady and knight,—that untroubled and sacred sky, which was to all men, in those days of innocent faith, indeed the unquestioned abode of spirits, as the earth was of men; and which opened straight through its gates of cloud and veils of dew into the awfulness of the eternal world;—a heaven in which every cloud that passed was literally the chariot of an angel, and every ray of its Evening and Morning streamed from the throne of God.

What think you of that for a school of design?

I do not bring this contrast before you as a ground of hopelessness in our task; neither do I look for any possible renovation of the Republic of Pisa, at Bradford, in the nineteenth century; but I put it before you in order that you may be aware precisely of the kind of difficulty you have to meet, and may then consider with yourselves how far you can meet it. To men surrounded by the depressing and monotonous circumstances of English manufacturing life, depend upon it, design is simply impossible. This is the most distinct of all the experiences I have had in dealing with the modern workman. He is intelligent and ingenious in the highest degree—subtle in touch and keen in sight: but he is, generally speaking, wholly destitute of designing power. And if you want to give him the power, you must give him the materials, and put him in the circumstances for it. Design is not the offspring of idle fancy: it is the studied result of accumulative observation and delightful habit. Without observation and experience, no design— without peace and pleasurableness in occupation, no design—and all the lecturings, and teachings, and prizes, and principles of art, in the world, are of no use, so long as you don't surround your men with happy influences and beautiful things. It is impossible for them to have right ideas about colour, unless they see the lovely colours of nature unspoiled; impossible for them to supply beautiful incident and action in their ornament, unless they see beautiful incident and action in the world about them. Inform their minds, refine their habits, and you form and refine their designs; but keep them illiterate, uncomfortable, and in the midst of unbeautiful things, and whatever they do will still be spurious, vulgar, and valueless.

I repeat, that I do not ask you nor wish you to build a new Pisa for them. We don't want either the life or the decorations of the thirteenth century back again; and the circumstances with which you must surround your workmen are those simply of happy modern English life, because the designs you have now to ask for from your workmen are such as will make modern English life beautiful. All that gorgeousness of the middle ages, beautiful as it sounds in description, noble as in many respects it was in reality, had, nevertheless, for foundation and for end, nothing but the pride of life—the pride of the so-called superior classes; a pride which supported itself by violence and robbery, and led in the end to the destruction both of the arts themselves and the States in which they nourished.

The great lesson of history is, that all the fine arts hitherto—having been supported by the selfish power of the noblesse, and never having extended their range to the comfort or the relief of the mass of the people—the arts, I say, thus practised, and thus matured, have only accelerated the ruin of the States they adorned; and at the moment when, in any kingdom, you point to the triumphs of its greatest artists, you point also to the determined hour of the kingdom's decline. The names of great painters are like passing bells: in the name of Velasquez, you hear sounded the fall of Spain; in the name of Titian, that of Venice; in the name of Leonardo, that of Milan; in the name of Raphael, that of Rome. And there is profound justice in this; for in proportion to the nobleness of the power is the guilt of its use for purposes vain or vile; and hitherto the greater the art, the more surely has it been used, and used solely, for the decoration of pride, [Footnote: Whether religious or profane pride,—chapel or banqueting room,—is no matter.] or the provoking of sensuality. Another course lies open to us. We may abandon the hope—or if you like the words better—we may disdain the temptation, of the pomp and grace of Italy in her youth. For us there can be no more the throne of marble—for us no more the vault of gold—but for us there is the loftier and lovelier privilege of bringing the power and charm of art within the reach of the humble and the poor; and as the magnificence of past ages failed by its narrowness and its pride, ours may prevail and continue, by its universality and its lowliness.

And thus, between the picture of too laborious England, which we imagined as future, and the picture of too luxurious Italy, which we remember in the past, there may exist—there will exist, if we do our duty—an intermediate condition, neither oppressed by labour nor wasted in vanity—the condition of a peaceful and thoughtful temperance in aims, and acts, and arts.

We are about to enter upon a period of our world's history in which domestic life, aided by the arts of peace, will slowly, but at last entirely, supersede public life and the arts of war. For our own England, she will not, I believe, be blasted throughout with furnaces; nor will she be encumbered with palaces. I trust she will keep her green fields, her cottages, and her homes of middle life; but these ought to be, and I trust will be enriched with a useful, truthful, substantial form of art. We want now no more feasts of the gods, nor martyrdoms of the saints; we have no need of sensuality, no place for superstition, or for costly insolence. Let us have learned and faithful historical painting— touching and thoughtful representations of human nature, in dramatic painting; poetical and familiar renderings of natural objects and of landscape; and rational, deeply-felt realizations of the events which are the subjects of our religious faith. And let these things we want, as far as possible, be scattered abroad and made accessible to all men.

So also, in manufacture: we require work substantial rather than rich in make; and refined, rather than splendid in design. Your stuffs need not be such as would catch the eye of a duchess; but they should be such as may at once serve the need, and refine the taste, of a cottager. The prevailing error in English dress, especially among the lower orders, is a tendency to flimsiness and gaudiness, arising mainly from the awkward imitation of their superiors. [Footnote: If their superiors would give them simplicity and economy to imitate, it would, in the issue, be well for themselves, as well as for those whom they guide. The typhoid fever of passion for dress, and all other display, which has struck the upper classes of Europe at this time, is one of the most dangerous political elements we have to deal with. Its wickedness I have shown elsewhere (Polit. Economy of Art, p. 62, *et seq.*); but its wickedness is, in the minds of most persons, a matter of no importance. I wish I had time also to show them its danger. I cannot enter here into political investigation; but this is a certain fact, that the wasteful and vain expenses at present indulged in by the upper classes are hastening the advance of republicanism more than any other element of modern change. No agitators, no clubs, no epidemical errors, ever were, or will be, fatal to social order in any nation. Nothing but the guilt of the upper classes, wanton, accumulated, reckless, and merciless, ever overthrows them Of such guilt they have now much to answer for—let them look to it in time.] It should be one of the first objects of all manufacturers to produce stuffs not only beautiful and quaint in design, but also adapted for every-day service, and decorous in humble and secluded life. And you must remember always that your business, as manufacturers, is to form the market, as much as to supply it. If, in shortsighted and reckless eagerness for wealth, you catch at every humour of the populace as it shapes itself into momentary demand—if, in jealous rivalry with neighbouring States, or with other producers, you try to attract attention by singularities, novelties, and gaudinesses—to make every design an advertisement, and pilfer every idea of a successful neighbour's, that you may insidiously imitate it, or pompously eclipse —no good design will ever be possible to you, or perceived by you. You may, by accident, snatch the market; or, by energy, command it; you may obtain the confidence of the public, and cause the ruin of opponent houses; or you may, with equal justice of fortune, be ruined by them. But whatever happens to you, this, at least, is certain, that the whole of your life will have been spent in corrupting public taste and encouraging public extravagance. Every preference you have won by gaudiness must have been based on the purchaser's vanity; every demand you have created by novelty has fostered in the consumer a habit of discontent; and when you retire into inactive life, you may, as a subject of consolation for your declining years, reflect that precisely according to the extent of your past operations, your life has been successful in retarding the arts,—tarnishing the virtues, and confusing the manners of your country.

But, on the other hand, if you resolve from the first that, so far as you can ascertain or discern what is best, you will produce what is best, on an intelligent consideration of the probable tendencies and possible tastes of the people whom you supply, you may literally become more influential for all kinds of good than many lecturers on art, or many treatise-writers on morality. Considering the materials dealt with, and the crude state of art knowledge at the time, I do not know that any more wide or effective influence in public taste was ever exercised than that of the Staffordshire manufacture of pottery under William Wedgwood, and it only rests with the manufacturer in every other business to determine whether he will, in like manner, make his wares educational instruments, or mere drugs of the market. You all should, be, in a certain sense, authors: you must, indeed, first catch the public eye, as an author must the public ear; but once gain your audience, or observance, and as it is in the writer's power thenceforward to publish what will educate as it amuses—so it is in yours to publish what will educate as it adorns. Nor is this surely a subject of poor ambition. I hear it said continually that men are too ambitious: alas! to me, it seems they are never enough ambitious. How many are content to be merely the thriving merchants of a state, when they might be its guides, counsellors, and rulers—wielding powers of subtle but gigantic beneficence, in restraining its follies while they supplied its wants. Let such duty, such ambition, be once accepted in their fulness, and the best glory of European art and of European manufacture may yet be to come. The paintings of Raphael and of Buonaroti gave force to the falsehoods of superstition, and majesty to the imaginations of sin; but the arts of England may have, for their task, to inform the soul with truth, and touch the heart with compassion. The steel of Toledo and the silk of Genoa did but give strength to oppression and lustre to pride: let it be for the furnace and for the loom of England, as they have already richly earned, still more abundantly to bestow, comfort on the indigent, civilization on the rude, and to dispense, through the peaceful homes of nations, the grace and the preciousness of simple adornment, and useful possession.

LECTURE IV.

INFLUENCE OF IMAGINATION IN ARCHITECTURE

An Address Delivered to the Members of the Architectural Association, in Lyon's Inn Hall, 1857.

If we were to be asked abruptly, and required to answer briefly, what qualities chiefly distinguish great artists from feeble artists, we should answer, I suppose, first, their sensibility and tenderness; secondly, their imagination; and thirdly, their industry. Some of us might, perhaps, doubt the justice of attaching so much importance to this last character, because we have all known clever men who were indolent, and dull men who were industrious. But though you may have known clever men who were indolent, you never knew a great man who was so; and, during such investigation as I have been able to give to the lives of the artists whose works are in all points noblest, no fact ever looms so large upon me—no law remains so steadfast in the universality of its application, as the fact and law that they are all great workers: nothing concerning them is matter of more astonishment than the quantity they have accomplished in the given length of their life; and when I hear a young man spoken of, as giving promise of high genius, the first question I ask about him is always—

Does he work?

But though this quality of industry is essential to an artist, it does not in anywise make an artist; many people are busy, whose doings are little worth. Neither does sensibility make an artist; since, as I hope, many can feel both strongly and nobly, who yet care nothing about art. But the gifts which distinctively mark the artist—*without* which he must be feeble in life, forgotten in death—*with* which he may become

one of the shakers of the earth, and one of the signal lights in heaven—
are those of sympathy and imagination. I will not occupy your time,
nor incur the risk of your dissent, by endeavouring to give any close
definition of this last word. We all have a general and sufficient idea
of imagination, and of its work with our hands and in our hearts: we
understand it, I suppose, as the imaging or picturing of new things
in our thoughts; and we always show an involuntary respect for
this power, wherever we can recognize it, acknowledging it to be a
greater power than manipulation, or calculation, or observation, or
any other human faculty. If we see an old woman spinning at the
fireside, and distributing her thread dexterously from the distaff,
we respect her for her manipulation—if we ask her how much she
expects to make in a year, and she answers quickly, we respect her for
her calculation—if she is watching at the same time that none of her
grandchildren fall into the fire, we respect her for her observation—
yet for all this she may still be a commonplace old woman enough.
But if she is all the time telling her grandchildren a fairy tale out of
her head, we praise her for her imagination, and say, she must be a
rather remarkable old woman. Precisely in like manner, if an architect
does his working-drawing well, we praise him for his manipulation—
if he keeps closely within his contract, we praise him for his honest
arithmetic—if he looks well to the laying of his beams, so that nobody
shall drop through the floor, we praise him for his observation. But
he must, somehow, tell us a fairy tale out of his head beside all this,
else we cannot praise him for his imagination, nor speak of him as we
did of the old woman, as being in any wise out of the common way, a
rather remarkable architect. It seemed to me, therefore, as if it might
interest you to-night, if we were to consider together what fairy tales
are, in and by architecture, to be told—what there is for you to do in
this severe art of yours "out of your heads," as well as by your hands.

Perhaps the first idea which a young architect is apt to be allured by,
as a head-problem in these experimental days, is its being incumbent
upon him to invent a "new style" worthy of modern civilization in
general, and of England in particular; a style worthy of our engines
and telegraphs; as expansive as steam, and as sparkling as electricity.

But, if there are any of my hearers who have been impressed
with this sense of inventive duty, may I ask them first, whether their
plan is that every inventive architect among us shall invent a new

style for himself, and have a county set aside for his conceptions, or a province for his practice? Or, must every architect invent a little piece of the new style, and all put it together at last like a dissected map? And if so, when the new style is invented, what is to be done next? I will grant you this Eldorado of imagination—but can you have more than one Columbus? Or, if you sail in company, and divide the prize of your discovery and the honour thereof, who is to come after you clustered Columbuses? to what fortunate islands of style are your architectural descendants to sail, avaricious of new lands? When our desired style is invented, will not the best we can all do be simply—to build in it?— and cannot you now do that in styles that are known? Observe, I grant, for the sake of your argument, what perhaps many of you know that I would not grant otherwise—that a new style *can* be invented. I grant you not only this, but that it shall be wholly different from any that was ever practised before. We will suppose that capitals are to be at the bottom of pillars instead of the top; and that buttresses shall be on the tops of pinnacles instead of at the bottom; that you roof your apertures with stones which shall neither be arched nor horizontal; and that you compose your decoration of lines which shall neither be crooked nor straight. The furnace and the forge shall be at your service: you shall draw out your plates of glass and beat out your bars of iron till you have encompassed us all,—if your style is of the practical kind,—with endless perspective of black skeleton and blinding square,—or if your style is to be of the ideal kind—you shall wreathe your streets with ductile leafage, and roof them with variegated crystal—you shall put, if you will, all London under one blazing dome of many colours that shall light the clouds round it with its flashing, as far as to the sea. And still, I ask you, What after this? Do you suppose those imaginations of yours will ever lie down there asleep beneath the shade of your iron leafage, or within the coloured light of your enchanted dome? Not so. Those souls, and fancies, and ambitions of yours, are wholly infinite; and, whatever may be done by others, you will still want to do something for yourselves; if you cannot rest content with Palladio, neither will you with Paxton: all the metal and glass that ever were melted have not so much weight in them as will clog the wings of one human spirit's aspiration.

If you will think over this quietly by yourselves, and can get the noise out of your ears of the perpetual, empty, idle, incomparably idiotic talk about the necessity of some novelty in architecture, you will soon see that the very essence of a Style, properly so called, is that it should be practised *for ages*, and applied to all purposes; and that so long as any given style is in practice, all that is left for individual imagination to accomplish must be within the scope of that style, not in the invention of a new one. If there are any here, therefore, who hope to obtain celebrity by the invention of some strange way of building which must convince all Europe into its adoption, to them, for the moment, I must not be understood to address myself, but only to those who would be content with that degree of celebrity which an artist may enjoy who works in the manner of his forefathers;—which the builder of Salisbury Cathedral might enjoy in England, though he did not invent Gothic; and which Titian might enjoy at Venice, though he did not invent oil painting. Addressing myself then to those humbler, but wiser, or rather, only wise students who are content to avail themselves of some system of building already understood, let us consider together what room for the exercise of the imagination may be left to us under such conditions. And, first, I suppose it will be said, or thought, that the architect's principal field for exercise of his invention must be in the disposition of lines, mouldings, and masses, in agreeable proportions. Indeed, if you adopt some styles of architecture, you cannot exercise invention in any other way. And I admit that it requires genius and special gift to do this rightly. Not by rule, nor by study, can the gift of graceful proportionate design be obtained; only by the intuition of genius can so much as a single tier of façade be beautifully arranged; and the man has just cause for pride, as far as our gifts can ever be a cause for pride, who finds himself able, in a design of his own, to rival even the simplest arrangement of parts in one by Sanmicheli, Inigo Jones, or Christopher Wren.

Invention, then, and genius being granted, as necessary to accomplish this, let me ask you, What, after all, with this special gift and genius, you *have* accomplished, when you have arranged the lines of a building beautifully?

In the first place you will not, I think, tell me that the beauty there attained is of a touching or pathetic kind. A well-disposed group of notes in music will make you sometimes weep and sometimes laugh. You can express the depth of all affections by those dispositions of sound: you can give courage to the soldier, language to the lover, consolation to the mourner, more joy to the joyful, more humility to the devout. Can you do as much by your group of lines? Do you suppose the front of Whitehall, a singularly beautiful one ever inspires the two Horse Guards, during the hour they sit opposite to it, with military ardour? Do you think that the lovers in our London walk down to the front of Whitehall for consolation when mistresses are unkind; or that any person wavering in duty, or feeble in faith, was ever confirmed in purpose or in creed by the pathetic appeal of those harmonious architraves? You will not say so. Then, if they cannot touch, or inspire, or comfort any one, can your architectural proportions amuse any one? Christmas is just over; you have doubtless been at many merry parties during the period. Can you remember any in which architectural proportions contributed to the entertainment of the evening? Proportions of notes in music were, I am sure, essential to your amusement; the setting of flowers in hair, and of ribands on dresses, were also subjects of frequent admiration with you, not inessential to your happiness. Among the juvenile members of your society the proportion of currants in cake, and of sugar in comfits, became subjects of acute interest; and, when such proportions were harmonious, motives also of gratitude to cook and to confectioner. But did you ever see either young or old amused by the architrave of the door? Or otherwise interested in the proportions of the room than as they admitted more or fewer friendly faces? Nay, if all the amusement that there is in the best proportioned architecture of London could be concentrated into one evening, and you were to issue tickets for nothing to this great proportional entertainment;—how do you think it would stand between you and the Drury pantomine?

You are, then, remember, granted to be people of genius—great and admirable; and you devote your lives to your art, but you admit that you cannot comfort anybody, you cannot encourage anybody, you cannot improve anybody, and you cannot amuse anybody. I proceed then farther to ask, Can you inform anybody? Many sciences cannot be considered as highly touching or emotional; nay, perhaps not specially amusing; scientific men may sometimes, in these respects, stand on the same ground with you. As far as we can judge by the results of the late war, science helps our soldiers about as much as the front of Whitehall; and at the Christmas parties, the children wanted no geologists to tell them about the behaviour of bears and dragons in Queen Elizabeth's time. Still, your man of science teaches you something; he may be dull at a party, or helpless in a battle, he is not always that; but he can give you, at all events, knowledge of noble facts, and open to you the secrets of the earth and air. Will your architectural proportions do as much? Your genius is granted, and your life is given, and what do you teach us?—Nothing, I believe, from one end of that life to the other, but that two and two make four, and that one is to two as three is to six.

You cannot, then, it is admitted, comfort any one, serve or amuse any one, nor teach any one. Finally, I ask, Can you be of *Use* to any one? «Yes,» you reply; «certainly we are of some use—we architects—in a climate like this, where it always rains." You are of use certainly; but, pardon me, only as builders—not as proportionalists. We are not talking of building as a protection, but only of that special work which your genius is to do; not of building substantial and comfortable houses like Mr. Cubitt, but of putting beautiful façades on them like Inigo Jones. And, again, I ask—Are you of use to any one? Will your proportions of the façade heal the sick, or clothe the naked? Supposing you devoted your lives to be merchants, you might reflect at the close of them, how many, fainting for want, you had brought corn to sustain; how many, infected with disease, you had brought balms to heal; how widely, among multitudes of far-away nations, you had scattered the first seeds of national power, and guided the first rays of sacred light. Had you been, in fine, *anything* else in the world *but* architectural designers, you might have been of some use or good to people. Content to be petty tradesmen, you would have saved the time of mankind;—rough-handed daily labourers, you would have added to their stock of food or of clothing. But, being men of genius, and devoting your lives to the exquisite exposition of this genius, on what achievements do you think the memories of your old age are to fasten? Whose gratitude will surround you with its glow, or on what accomplished good, of that greatest kind for which men show *no* gratitude, will your life rest the contentment of its close? Truly, I fear that the ghosts of proportionate lines will be thin phantoms at your bedsides—very speechless to you; and that on all the emanations of your high genius you will look back with less delight than you might have done on a cup of cold water given to him who was thirsty, or to a single moment when you had "prevented with your bread him that fled."

Do not answer, nor think to answer, that with your great works and great payments of workmen in them, you would do this; I know you would, and will, as Builders; but, I repeat, it is not your *building* that I am talking about, but your *brains*; it is your invention and imagination of whose profit I am speaking. The good done through the building, observe, is done by your employers, not by you—you share in the benefit of it. The good that *you* personally must do is by your designing; and I compare you with musicians who do good by their pathetic composing, not as they do good by employing fiddlers in the orchestra; for it is the public who in reality do that, not the musicians. So clearly keeping to this one question, what good we architects are to do by our genius; and having found that on our proportionate system we can do no good to others, will you tell me, lastly, what good we can do to *ourselves*?

Observe, nearly every other liberal art or profession has some intense pleasure connected with it, irrespective of any good to others. As lawyers, or physicians, or clergymen, you would have the pleasure of investigation, and of historical reading, as part of your work: as men of science you would be rejoicing in curiosity perpetually gratified respecting the laws and facts of nature: as artists you would have delight in watching the external forms of nature: as day labourers or petty tradesmen, supposing you to undertake such work with as much intellect as you are going to devote to your designing, you would find continued subjects of interest in the manufacture or the agriculture which you helped to improve; or in the problems of commerce which bore on your business. But your architectural designing leads you into no pleasant journeys,—into no seeing of lovely things,—no discerning of just laws,—no warmths of compassion, no humilities of veneration, no progressive state of sight or soul. Our conclusion is—must be—that you will not amuse, nor inform, nor help anybody; you will not amuse, nor better, nor inform yourselves; you will sink into a state in which you can neither show, nor feel, nor see, anything, but that one is to two as three is to six. And in that state what should we call ourselves? Men? I think not. The right name for us would be— numerators and denominators. Vulgar Fractions.

Shall we, then, abandon this theory of the soul of architecture being in proportional lines, and look whether we can find anything better to exert our fancies upon?

May we not, to begin with, accept this great principle—that, as our bodies, to be in health, must be *generally* exercised, so our minds, to be in health, must be *generally* cultivated? You would not call a man healthy who had strong arms but was paralytic in his feet; nor one who could walk well, but had no use of his hands; nor one who could see well, if he could not hear. You would not voluntarily reduce your bodies to any such partially developed state. Much more, then, you would not, if you could help it, reduce your minds to it. Now, your minds are endowed with a vast number of gifts of totally different uses—limbs of mind as it were, which, if you don't exercise, you cripple. One is curiosity; that is a gift, a capacity of pleasure in knowing; which if you destroy, you make yourselves cold and dull. Another is sympathy; the power of sharing in the feelings of living creatures, which if you destroy, you make yourselves hard and cruel. Another of your limbs of mind is admiration; the power of enjoying beauty or ingenuity, which, if you destroy, you make yourselves base and irreverent. Another is wit; or the power of playing with the lights on the many sides of truth; which if you destroy, you make yourselves gloomy, and less useful and cheering to others than you might be. So that in choosing your way of work it should be your aim, as far as possible, to bring out all these faculties, as far as they exist in you; not one merely, nor another, but all of them. And the way to bring them out, is simply to concern yourselves attentively with the subjects of each faculty. To cultivate sympathy you must be among living creatures, and thinking about them; and to cultivate admiration, you must be among beautiful things and looking at them.

All this sounds much like truism, at least I hope it does, for then you will surely not refuse to act upon it; and to consider farther, how, as architects, you are to keep yourselves in contemplation of living creatures and lovely things.

You all probably know the beautiful photographs which have been published within the last year or two of the porches of the Cathedral of Amiens. I hold one of these up to you, (merely that you may know what I am talking about, as of course you cannot see the detail at this distance, but you will recognise the subject.) Have you ever considered how much sympathy, and how much humour, are developed in filling this single doorway [Footnote: The tympanum of the south transcept door; it is to be found generally among all collections of architectural photographs] with these sculptures of the history of St. Honoré (and, by the way, considering how often we English are now driving up and down the Rue St. Honoré, we may as well know as much of the saint as the old architect cared to tell us). You know in all legends of saints who ever were bishops, the first thing you are told of them is that they didn't want to be bishops. So here is St. Honoré, who doesn't want to be a bishop, sitting sulkily in the corner; he hugs his book with both hands, and won't get up to take his crosier; and here are all the city aldermen of Amiens come to *poke* him up; and all the monks in the town in a great puzzle what they shall do for a bishop if St. Honoré won›t be; and here›s one of the monks in the opposite corner who is quite cool about it, and thinks they'll get on well enough without St Honoré,—you see that in his face perfectly. At last St. Honoré consents to be bishop, and here he sits in a throne, and has his book now grandly on his desk instead of his knees, and he directs one of his village curates how to find relics in a wood; here is the wood, and here is the village curate, and here are the tombs, with the bones of St. Victorien and Gentien in them.

After this, St. Honoré performs grand mass, and the miracle occurs of the appearance of a hand blessing the wafer, which occurrence afterwards was painted for the arms of the abbey. Then St. Honoré dies; and here is his tomb with his statue on the top; and miracles are being performed at it—a deaf man having his ear touched, and a blind man groping his way up to the tomb with his dog. Then here is a great procession in honour of the relics of St. Honoré; and under his coffin are some cripples being healed; and the coffin itself is put above the bar which separates the cross from the lower subjects, because the tradition is that the figure on the crucifix of the Church of St. Firmin bowed its head in token of acceptance, as the relics of St. Honoré passed beneath.

Now just consider the amount of sympathy with human nature, and observance of it, shown in this one bas-relief; the sympathy with disputing monks, with puzzled aldermen, with melancholy recluse, with triumphant prelate, with palsy-stricken poverty, with ecclesiastical magnificence, or miracle-working faith. Consider how much intellect was needed in the architect, and how much observance of nature before he could give the expression to these various figures—cast these multitudinous draperies—design these rich and quaint fragments of tombs and altars—weave with perfect animation the entangled branches of the forest.

But you will answer me, all this is not architecture at all—it is sculpture. Will you then tell me precisely where the separation exists between one and the other? We will begin at the very beginning. I will show you a piece of what you will certainly admit to be a piece of pure architecture; [Footnote: See Appendix III., "Classical Architecture."] it is drawn on the back of another photograph, another of these marvellous tympana from Notre Dame, which you call, I suppose, impure. Well, look on this picture, and on this. Don't laugh; you must not laugh, that's very improper of you, this is classical architecture. I have taken it out of the essay on that subject in the "Encyclopédia Britannica."

Yet I suppose none of you would think yourselves particularly ingenious architects if you had designed nothing more than this; nay, I will even let you improve it into any grand proportion you choose, and add to it as many windows as you choose; the only thing I insist upon in our specimen of pure architecture is, that there shall be no mouldings nor ornaments upon it. And I suspect you don't quite like your architecture so "pure" as this. We want a few mouldings, you will say—just a few. Those who want mouldings, hold up their hands. We are unanimous, I think. Will, you, then, design the profiles of these mouldings yourselves, or will you copy them? If you wish to copy them, and to copy them always, of course I leave you at once to your authorities, and your imaginations to their repose. But if you wish to design them yourselves, how do you do it? You draw the profile according to your taste, and you order your mason to cut it. Now, will you tell me the logical difference between drawing the profile of a moulding and giving *that* to be cut, and drawing the folds of the drapery of a statue and giving *those* to be cut. The last is much more difficult to do than the first; but degrees of difficulty constitute no specific difference, and you will not accept it, surely, as a definition of the difference between architecture and sculpture, that "architecture is doing anything that is easy, and sculpture anything that is difficult."

It is true, also, that the carved moulding represents nothing, and the carved drapery represents something; but you will not, I should think, accept, as an explanation of the difference between architecture and sculpture, this any more than the other, that "sculpture is art which has meaning, and architecture art which has none."

Where, then, is your difference? In this, perhaps, you will say; that whatever ornaments we can direct ourselves, and get accurately cut to order, we consider architectural. The ornaments that we are obliged to leave to the pleasure of the workman, or the superintendence of some other designer, we consider sculptural, especially if they are more or less extraneous and incrusted—not an essential part of the building.

Accepting this definition, I am compelled to reply, that it is in effect nothing more than an amplification of my first one—that whatever is easy you call architecture, whatever is difficult you call sculpture. For you cannot suppose the arrangement of the place in which the sculpture is to be put is so difficult or so great a part of the design as the sculpture itself. For instance: you all know the pulpit of Niccolo Pisano, in the baptistry at Pisa. It is composed of seven rich *relievi*, surrounded by panel mouldings, and sustained on marble shafts. Do you suppose Niccolo Pisano's reputation—such part of it at least as rests on this pulpit (and much does)—depends on the panel mouldings, or on the relievi? The panel mouldings are by his hand; he would have disdained to leave even them to a common workman; but do you think he found any difficulty in them, or thought there was any credit in them? Having once done the sculpture, those enclosing lines were mere child's play to him; the determination of the diameter of shafts and height of capitals was an affair of minutes; his *work* was in carving the Crucifixion and the Baptism.

Or, again, do you recollect Orcagna's tabernacle in the church of San Michele, at Florence? That, also, consists of rich and multitudinous bas-reliefs, enclosed in panel mouldings, with shafts of mosaic, and foliated arches sustaining the canopy. Do you think Orcagna, any more than Pisano, if his spirit could rise in the midst of us at this moment, would tell us that he had trusted his fame to the foliation, or had put his soul's pride into the panelling? Not so; he would tell you that his spirit was in the stooping figures that stand round the couch of the dying Virgin.

Or, lastly, do you think the man who designed the procession on the portal of Amiens was the subordinate workman? that there was an architect over *him*, restraining him within certain limits, and ordering of him his bishops at so much a mitre, and his cripples at so much a crutch? Not so. *Here*, on this sculptured shield, rests the Master's hand; *this* is the centre of the Master›s thought; from this, and in subordination to this, waved the arch and sprang the pinnacle. Having done this, and being able to give human expression and action to the stone, all the rest—the rib, the niche, the foil, the shaft—were mere toys to his hand and accessories to his conception: and if once you also gain the gift of doing this, if once you can carve one fronton such as you have here, I tell you, you would be able—so far as it depended on your invention—to scatter cathedrals over England as fast as clouds rise from its streams after summer rain.

Nay, but perhaps you answer again, our sculptors at present do not design cathedrals, and could not. No, they could not; but that is merely because we have made architecture so dull that they cannot take any interest in it, and, therefore, do not care to add to their higher knowledge the poor and common knowledge of principles of building. You have thus separated building from sculpture, and you have taken away the power of both; for the sculptor loses nearly as much by never having room for the development of a continuous work, as you do from having reduced your work to a continuity of mechanism. You are essentially, and should always be, the same body of men, admitting only such difference in operation as there is between the work of a painter at different times, who sometimes labours on a small picture, and sometimes on the frescoes of a palace gallery.

This conclusion, then, we arrive at, *must* arrive at; the fact being irrevocably so:—that in order to give your imagination and the other powers of your souls full play, you must do as all the great architects of old time did—you must yourselves be your sculptors. Phidias, Michael Angelo, Orcagna, Pisano, Giotto,—which of these men, do you think, could not use his chisel? You say, "It is difficult; quite out of your way." I know it is; nothing that is great is easy; and nothing that is great, so long as you study building without sculpture, can be *in* your way. I want to put it in your way, and you to find your way to it. But, on the other hand, do not shrink from the task as if the refined art of perfect sculpture were always required from you.

For, though architecture and sculpture are not separate arts, there is an architectural *manner* of sculpture; and it is, in the majority of its applications, a comparatively easy one. Our great mistake at present, in dealing with stone at all, is requiring to have all our work too refined; it is just the same mistake as if we were to require all our book illustrations to be as fine work as Raphael's. John Leech does not sketch so well as Leonardo da Vinci; but do you think that the public could easily spare him; or that he is wrong in bringing out his talent in the way in which it is most effective? Would you advise him, if he asked your advice, to give up his wood-blocks and take to canvas? I know you would not; neither would you tell him, I believe, on the other hand, that because he could not draw as well as Leonardo, therefore he ought to draw nothing but straight lines with a ruler, and circles with compasses, and no figure- subjects at all. That would be some loss to you; would it not? You would all be vexed if next week's *Punch* had nothing in it but proportionate lines. And yet, do not you see that you are doing precisely the same thing with *your* powers of sculptural design that he would be doing with his powers of pictorial design, if he gave you nothing but such lines. You feel that you cannot carve like Phidias; therefore you will not carve at all, but only draw mouldings; and thus all that intermediate power which is of especial value in modern days,—that popular power of expression which is within the attainment of thousands,—and would address itself to tens of thousands,—is utterly lost to us in stone, though in ink and paper it has become one of the most desired luxuries of modern civilization.

Here, then, is one part of the subject to which I would especially invite your attention, namely, the distinctive character which may be wisely permitted to belong to architectural sculpture, as distinguished from perfect sculpture on one side, and from mere geometrical decoration on the other.

And first, observe what an indulgence we have in the distance at which most work is to be seen. Supposing we were able to carve eyes and lips with the most exquisite precision, it would all be of no use as soon as the work was put far above the eye; but, on the other hand, as beauties disappear by being far withdrawn, so will faults; and the mystery and confusion which are the natural consequence of distance, while they would often render your best skill but vain, will as often render your worst errors of little consequence; nay, more than this, often a deep cut, or a rude angle, will produce in certain positions an effect of expression both startling and true, which you never hoped for. Not that mere distance will give animation to the work, if it has none in itself; but if it has life at all, the distance will make that life more perceptible and powerful by softening the defects of execution. So that you are placed, as workmen, in this position of singular advantage, that you may give your fancies free play, and strike hard for the expression that you want, knowing that, if you miss it, no one will detect you; if you at all touch it, nature herself will help you, and with every changing shadow and basking sunbeam bring forth new phases of your fancy.

But it is not merely this privilege of being imperfect which belongs to architectural sculpture. It has a true privilege of imagination, far excelling all that can be granted to the more finished work, which, for the sake of distinction, I will call,—and I don't think we can have a much better term—"furniture sculpture;" sculpture, that is, which can be moved from place to furnish rooms.

For observe, to that sculpture the spectator is usually brought in a tranquil or prosaic state of mind; he sees it associated rather with what is sumptuous than sublime, and under circumstances which address themselves more to his comfort than his curiosity. The statue which is to be pathetic, seen between the flashes of footmen's livery round the dining-table, must have strong elements of pathos in itself; and the statue which is to be awful, in the midst of the gossip of the drawing- room, must have the elements of awe wholly in itself. But the spectator is brought to *your* work already in an excited and imaginative mood. He has been impressed by the cathedral wall as it loomed over the low streets, before he looks up to the carving of its porch—and his love of mystery has been touched by the silence and the shadows of the cloister, before he can set himself to decipher the bosses on its vaulting. So that when once he begins to observe your doings, he will ask nothing better from you, nothing kinder from you, than that you would meet this imaginative temper of his half way;—that you would farther touch the sense of terror, or satisfy the expectation of things strange, which have been prompted by the mystery or the majesty of the surrounding scene. And thus, your leaving forms more or less undefined, or carrying out your fancies, however extravagant, in grotesqueness of shadow or shape, will be for the most part in accordance with the temper of the observer; and he is likely, therefore, much more willingly to use his fancy to help your meanings, than his judgment to detect your faults.

Again. Remember that when the imagination and feelings are strongly excited, they will not only bear with strange things, but they will *look* into *minute* things with a delight quite unknown in hours of tranquillity. You surely must remember moments of your lives in which, under some strong excitement of feeling, all the details of visible objects presented themselves with a strange intensity and insistance, whether you would or no; urging themselves upon the mind, and thrust upon the eye, with a force of fascination which you could not refuse. Now, to a certain extent, the senses get into this state whenever the imagination is strongly excited. Things trivial at other times assume a dignity or significance which we cannot explain; but which is only the more attractive because inexplicable: and the powers of attention, quickened by the feverish excitement, fasten and feed upon the minutest circumstances of detail, and remotest traces of intention. So that what would at other times be felt as more or less mean or extraneous in a work of sculpture, and which would assuredly be offensive to the perfect taste in its moments of languor, or of critical judgment, will be grateful, and even sublime, when it meets this frightened inquisitiveness, this fascinated watchfulness, of the roused imagination. And this is all for your advantage; for, in the beginnings of your sculpture, you will assuredly find it easier to imitate minute circumstances of costume or character, than to perfect the anatomy of simple forms or the flow of noble masses; and it will be encouraging to remember that the grace you cannot perfect, and the simplicity you cannot achieve, would be in great part vain, even if you could achieve them, in their appeal to the hasty curiosity of passionate fancy; but that the sympathy which would be refused to your science will be granted to your innocence: and that the mind of the general observer, though wholly unaffected by the correctness of anatomy or propriety of gesture, will follow you with fond and pleased concurrence, as you carve the knots of the hair, and the patterns of the vesture.

Farther yet. We are to remember that not only do the associated features of the larger architecture tend to excite the strength of fancy, but the architectural laws to which you are obliged to submit your decoration stimulate its *ingenuity*. Every crocket which you are to crest with sculpture,—every foliation which you have to fill, presents itself to the spectator's fancy, not only as a pretty thing, but as a *problematic* thing. It contained, he perceives immediately, not only a beauty which you wished to display, but a necessity which you were forced to meet; and the problem, how to occupy such and such a space with organic form in any probable way, or how to turn such a boss or ridge into a conceivable image of life, becomes at once, to him as to you, a matter of amusement as much as of admiration. The ordinary conditions of perfection in form, gesture, or feature, are willingly dispensed with, when the ugly dwarf and ungainly goblin have only to gather themselves into angles, or crouch to carry corbels; and the want of skill which, in other kinds of work would have been required for the finishing of the parts, will at once be forgiven here, if you have only disposed ingeniously what you have executed roughly, and atoned for the rudeness of your hands by the quickness of your wits.

Hitherto, however, we have been considering only the circumstances in architecture favourable to the development of the *powers* of imagination. A yet more important point for us seems, to me, the place which it gives to all the *objects* of imagination.

For, I suppose, you will not wish me to spend any time in proving, that imagination must be vigorous in proportion to the quantity of material which it has to handle; and that, just as we increase the range of what we see, we increase the richness of what we can imagine. Granting this, consider what a field is opened to your fancy merely in the subject matter which architecture admits. Nearly every other art is severely limited in its subjects—the landscape painter, for instance, gets little help from the aspects of beautiful humanity; the historical painter, less, perhaps, than he ought, from the accidents of wild nature; and the pure sculptor, still less, from the minor details of common life. But is there anything within range of sight, or conception, which may not be of use to *you*, or in which your interest may not be excited with advantage to your art? From visions of angels, down to the least important gesture of a child at play, whatever may be conceived of Divine, or beheld of Human, may be dared or adopted by you: throughout the kingdom of animal life, no creature is so vast, or so minute, that you cannot deal with it, or bring it into service; the lion and the crocodile will couch about your shafts; the moth and the bee will sun themselves upon your flowers; for you, the fawn will leap; for you, the snail be slow; for you, the dove smooth her bosom; and the hawk spread her wings toward the south. All the wide world of vegetation blooms and bends for you; the leaves tremble that you may bid them be still under the marble snow; the thorn and the thistle, which the earth casts forth as evil, are to you the kindliest servants; no dying petal, nor drooping tendril, is so feeble as to have no more help for you; no robed pride of blossom so kingly, but it will lay aside its purple to receive at your hands the pale immortality. Is there anything in common life too mean, — in common too trivial, — to be ennobled by your touch? As there is nothing in life, so there is nothing in lifelessness which has not its lesson for you, or its gift; and when you are tired of watching the strength of the plume, and the tenderness of the leaf, you may walk down to your rough river shore, or into the thickest markets of your thoroughfares, and there is not a piece of torn cable that will not twine into a perfect moulding; there is not a fragment of cast-away matting, or shattered basket-work, that will not work into a chequer or capital. Yes: and if you gather up the very sand, and break the stone on which you tread, among its fragments of all but invisible shells you will find forms that will take their place, and that proudly, among the starred traceries of your vaulting; and you, who can crown the mountain with its fortress, and the city with its towers, are thus able also to give beauty to ashes, and worthiness to dust.

Now, in that your art presents all this material to you, you have already much to rejoice in. But you have more to rejoice in, because all this is submitted to you, not to be dissected or analyzed, but to be sympathized with, and to bring out, therefore, what may be accurately called the moral part of imagination. We saw that, if we kept ourselves among lines only, we should have cause to envy the naturalist, because he was conversant with facts; but you will have little to envy now, if you make yourselves conversant with the feelings that arise out of his facts. For instance, the naturalist coming upon a block of marble, has to begin considering immediately how far its purple is owing to iron, or its whiteness to magnesia; he breaks his piece of marble, and at the close of his day, has nothing but a little sand in his crucible and some data added to the theory of the elements. But *you* approach your marble to sympathize with it, and rejoice over its beauty. You cut it a little indeed; but only to bring out its veins more perfectly; and at the end of your day's work you leave your marble shaft with joy and complacency in its perfectness, as marble. When you have to watch an animal instead of a stone, you differ from the naturalist in the same way. He may, perhaps, if he be an amiable naturalist, take delight in having living creatures round him;—still, the major part of his work is, or has been, in counting feathers, separating fibres, and analyzing structures. But *your* work is always with the living creature; the thing you have to get at in him is his life, and ways of going about things. It does not matter to you how many cells there are in his bones, or how many filaments in his feathers; what you want is his moral character and way of behaving himself; it is just that which your imagination, if healthy, will first seize—just that which your chisel, if vigorous, will first cut. You must get the storm spirit into your eagles, and the lordliness into your lions, and the tripping fear into your fawns; and in order to do this, you must be in continual sympathy with every fawn of them; and be hand-in-glove with all the lions, and hand-in-claw with all the hawks. And don't fancy that you will lower yourselves by sympathy with the lower creatures; you cannot sympathize rightly with the higher, unless you do with those: but you have to sympathize with the higher, too— with queens, and kings, and martyrs, and angels. Yes, and above all, and more than all, with simple humanity in all its needs and ways, for there is not one hurried face that passes you in the street that will not be impressive, if you can only fathom it. All history is open to you, all high thoughts and dreams that the past fortunes of men can suggest, all fairy land is open to you—no vision that ever haunted forest, or gleamed over hillside, but calls you to understand how it came into men's hearts, and may still touch them; and all Paradise is open to you—yes, and the work of Paradise; for in bringing all this, in perpetual and attractive truth, before the eyes of your fellow-men, you have to join in the employment of the angels, as well as to imagine their companies.

And observe, in this last respect, what a peculiar importance, and responsibility, are attached to your work, when you consider its permanence, and the multitudes to whom it is addressed. We frequently are led, by wise people, to consider what responsibility may sometimes attach to words, which yet, the chance is, will be heard by few, and forgotten as soon as heard. But none of *your* words will be heard by few, and none will be forgotten, for five or six hundred years, if you build well. You will talk to all who pass by; and all those little sympathies, those freaks of fancy, those jests in stone, those workings-out of problems in caprice, will occupy mind after mind of utterly countless multitudes, long after you are gone. You have not, like authors, to plead for a hearing, or to fear oblivion. Do but build large enough, and carve boldly enough, and all the world will hear you; they cannot choose but look.

I do not mean to awe you by this thought; I do not mean that because you will have so many witnesses and watchers, you are never to jest, or do anything gaily or lightly; on the contrary, I have pleaded, from the beginning, for this art of yours, especially because it has room for the whole of your character—if jest is in you, let the jest be jested; if mathematical ingenuity is yours, let your problem be put, and your solution worked out, as quaintly as you choose; above all, see that your work is easily and happily done, else it will never make anybody else happy; but while you thus give the rein to all your impulses, see that those impulses be headed and centred by one noble impulse; and let that be Love—triple love—for the art which you practise, the creation in which you move, and the creatures to whom you minister.

I. I say, first, Love for the art which you practise. Be assured that if ever any other motive becomes a leading one in your mind, as the principal one for exertion, except your love of art, that moment it is all over with your art. I do not say you are to desire money, nor to desire fame, nor to desire position; you cannot but desire all three; nay, you may—if you are willing that I should use the word Love in a desecrated sense—love all three; that is, passionately covet them, yet you must not covet or love them in the first place. Men of strong passions and imaginations must always care a great deal for anything they care for at all; but the whole question is one of first or second. Does your art lead you, or your gain lead you? You may like making money exceedingly; but if it come to a fair question, whether you are to make five hundred pounds less by this business, or to spoil your building, and you choose to spoil your building, there's an end of you. So you may be as thirsty for fame as a cricket is for cream; but, if it come to a fair question, whether you are to please the mob, or do the thing as you know it ought to be done; and you can't do both, and choose to please the mob, it's all over with you—there's no hope for you; nothing that you can do will ever be worth a man's glance as he passes by. The test is absolute, inevitable—Is your art first with you? Then you are artists; you may be, after you have made your money, misers and usurers; you may be, after you have got your fame, jealous, and proud, and wretched, and base: but yet, *as long as you won't spoil your work,* you are artists. On the other hand—Is your money first with you, and your fame first with you? Then, you may be very charitable with your money, and very magnificent with your money, and very graceful in the way you wear your reputation, and very courteous to those beneath you, and very acceptable to those above you; but you are *not artists.* You are mechanics, and drudges.

II. You must love the creation you work in the midst of. For, wholly in proportion to the intensity of feeling which you bring to the subject you have chosen, will be the depth and justice of our perception of its character. And this depth of feeling is not to be gained on the instant, when you want to bring it to bear on this or that. It is the result of the general habit of striving to feel rightly; and, among thousands of various means of doing this, perhaps the one I ought specially to name to you, is the keeping yourselves clear of petty and mean cares. Whatever you do, don't be anxious, nor fill your heads with little chagrins and little desires. I have just said, that you may be great artists, and yet be miserly and jealous, and troubled about many things. So you may be; but I said also that the miserliness or trouble must not be in your hearts all day. It is possible that you may get a habit of saving money; or it is possible, at a time of great trial, you may yield to the temptation of speaking unjustly of a rival,—and you will shorten your powers arid dim your sight even by this;—but the thing that you have to dread far more than any such unconscious habit, or—any such momentary fall—is the *constancy of small emotions;*—the anxiety whether Mr. So-and-so will like your work; whether such and such a workman will do all that you want of him, and so on;—not wrong feelings or anxieties in themselves, but impertinent, and wholly incompatible with the full exercise of your imagination.

Keep yourselves, therefore, quiet, peaceful, with your eyes open. It doesn't matter at all what Mr. So-and-so thinks of your work; but it matters a great deal what that bird is doing up there in its nest, or how that vagabond child at the street corner is managing his game of knuckle-down. And remember, you cannot turn aside from your own interests, to the birds' and the children's interests, unless you have long before got into the habit of loving and watching birds and children; so that it all comes at last to the forgetting yourselves, and the living out of yourselves, in the calm of the great world, or if you will, in its agitation; but always in a calm of your own bringing. Do not think it wasted time to submit yourselves to any influence which may bring upon you any noble feeling. Rise early, always watch the sunrise, and the way the clouds break from the dawn; you will cast your statue-draperies in quite another than your common way, when the remembrance of that cloud motion is with you, and of the scarlet vesture of the morning. Live always in the springtime in the country; you do not know what leaf-form means, unless you have seen the buds burst, and the young leaves breathing low in the sunshine, and wondering at the first shower of rain. But above all, accustom yourselves to look for, and to love, all nobleness of gesture and feature in the human form; and remember that the highest nobleness is usually among the aged, the poor, and the infirm; you will find, in the end, that it is not the strong arm of the soldier, nor the laugh of the young beauty, that are the best studies for you. Look at them, and look at them reverently; but be assured that endurance is nobler than strength, and patience than beauty; and that it is not in the high church pews, where the gay dresses are, but in the church free seats, where the widows' weeds are, that you may see the faces that will fit best between the angels' wings, in the church porch.

III. And therefore, lastly, and chiefly, you must love the creatures to whom you minister, your fellow-men; for, if you do not love them, not only will you be little interested in the passing events of life, but in all your gazing at humanity, you will be apt to be struck only by outside form, and not by expression. It is only kindness and tenderness which will ever enable you to see what beauty there is in the dark eyes that are sunk with weeping, and in the paleness of those fixed faces which the earth's adversity has compassed about, till they shine in their patience like dying watchfires through twilight. But it is not this only which makes it needful for you, if you would be great, to be also kind; there is a most important and all-essential reason in the very nature of your own art. So soon as you desire to build largely, and with addition of noble sculpture, you will find that your work must be associative. You cannot carve a whole cathedral yourself—you can carve but few and simple parts of it. Either your own work must be disgraced in the mass of the collateral inferiority, or you must raise your fellow-designers to correspondence of power. If you have genius, you will yourselves take the lead in the building you design; you will carve its porch and direct its disposition. But for all subsequent advancement of its detail, you must trust to the agency and the invention of others; and it rests with you either to repress what faculties your workmen have, into cunning subordination to your own; or to rejoice in discovering even the powers that may rival you, and leading forth mind after mind into fellowship with your fancy, and association with your fame.

I need not tell you that if you do the first—if you endeavour to depress or disguise the talents of your subordinates—you are lost; for nothing could imply more darkly and decisively than this, that your art and your work were not beloved by you; that it was your own prosperity that you were seeking, and your own skill only that you cared to contemplate. I do not say that you must not be jealous at all; it is rarely in human nature to be wholly without jealousy; and you may be forgiven for going some day sadly home, when you find some youth, unpractised and unapproved, giving the life-stroke to his work which you, after years of training, perhaps, cannot reach; but your jealousy must not conquer—your love of your building must conquer, helped by your kindness of heart. See—I set no high or difficult standard before you. I do not say that you are to surrender your pre-eminence in *mere* unselfish generosity. But I do say that you must surrender your pre-eminence in your love of your building helped by your kindness; and that whomsoever you find better able to do what will adorn it than you,—that person you are to give place to; and to console yourselves for the humiliation, first, by your joy in seeing the edifice grow more beautiful under his chisel, and secondly, by your sense of having done kindly and justly. But if you are morally strong enough to make the kindness and justice the first motive, it will be better;—best of all, if you do not consider it as kindness at all, but bare and stern justice; for, truly, such help as we can give each other in this world is a *debt* to each other; and the man who perceives a superiority or a capacity in a subordinate, and neither confesses, nor assists it, is not merely the withholder of kindness, but the committer of injury. But be the motive what you will, only see that you do the thing; and take the joy of the consciousness that, as your art embraces a wider field than all others—and addresses a vaster multitude than all others—and is surer of audience than all others—so it is profounder and holier in Fellowship than all others. The artist, when his pupil is perfect, must see him leave his side that he may declare his distinct, perhaps opponent, skill. Man of science wrestles with man of science for priority of discovery, and pursues in pangs of jealous haste his solitary inquiry. You alone are called by kindness,— by necessity,—by equity, to fraternity of toil; and thus, in those misty and massive piles which rise above the domestic roofs of our ancient cities, there was—there may be again—a meaning more profound and true than any that fancy so commonly has attached to them. Men say their pinnacles point to heaven. Why, so does every tree that buds, and every bird that rises as it sings. Men say their aisles are good for worship. Why, so is every mountain glen, and rough sea-shore. But this they have of distinct and indisputable glory,—that their mighty walls were never raised, and never shall be, but by men who love and aid each other in their weakness;—that all their interlacing strength of vaulted stone has its foundation upon the stronger arches of manly fellowship, and all their changing grace of depressed or lifted pinnacle owes its cadence and completeness to sweeter symmetries of human soul.

LECTURE V.

THE WORK OP IRON,
IN NATURE, ART, AND POLICY.

A Lecture Delivered at Tunbridge Wells, February, 1858.

When first I heard that you wished me to address you this evening, it was a matter of some doubt with me whether I could find any subject that would possess any sufficient interest for you to justify my bringing you out of your comfortable houses on a winter's night. When I venture to speak about my own special business of art, it is almost always before students of art, among whom I may sometimes permit myself to be dull, if I can feel that I am useful: but a mere talk about art, especially without examples to refer to (and I have been unable to prepare any careful illustrations for this lecture), is seldom of much interest to a general audience. As I was considering what you might best bear with me in speaking about, there came naturally into my mind a subject connected with the origin and present prosperity of the town you live in; and, it seemed to me, in the out-branchings of it, capable of a very general interest. When, long ago (I am afraid to think how long), Tunbridge Wells was my Switzerland, and I used to be brought down here in the summer, a sufficiently active child, rejoicing in the hope of clambering sandstone cliffs of stupendous height above the common, there used sometimes, as, I suppose, there are in the lives of all children at the Wells, to be dark days in my life—days of condemnation to the pantiles and band—under which calamities my only consolation used to be in watching, at every turn in my walk, the welling forth of the spring over the orange rim of its marble basin. The memory of the clear water, sparkling over its saffron stain, came back to me as the strongest image connected with the place; and it struck me that you might not be unwilling, to-night, to think a little over the full significance of that saffron stain, and of the power, in other ways and other functions, of the steelly element to which so many here owe returning strength and life;—chief as it has been always, and is yet more and more markedly so day by day, among the precious gifts of the earth.

The subject is, of course, too wide to be more than suggestively treated; and even my suggestions must be few, and drawn chiefly from my own fields of work; nevertheless, I think I shall have time to indicate some courses of thought which you may afterwards follow out for yourselves if they interest you; and so I will not shrink from the full scope of the subject which I have announced to you—the functions of Iron, in Nature, Art, and Policy.

Without more preface, I will take up the first head.

I. IRON IN NATURE.—You all probably know that the ochreous stain, which, perhaps, is often thought to spoil the basin of your spring, is iron in a state of rust: and when you see rusty iron in other places you generally think, not only that it spoils the places it stains, but that it is spoiled itself—that rusty iron is spoiled iron.

For most of our uses it generally is so; and because we cannot use a rusty knife or razor so well as a polished one, we suppose it to be a great defect in iron that it is subject to rust. But not at all. On the contrary, the most perfect and useful state of it is that ochreous stain; and therefore it is endowed with so ready a disposition to get itself into that state. It is not a fault in the iron, but a virtue, to be so fond of getting rusted, for in that condition it fulfils its most important functions in the universe, and most kindly duties to mankind. Nay, in a certain sense, and almost a literal one, we may say that iron rusted is Living; but when pure or polished, Dead. You all probably know that in the mixed air we breathe, the part of it essentially needful to us is called oxygen; and that this substance is to all animals, in the most accurate sense of the word, "breath of life." The nervous power of life is a different thing; but the supporting element of the breath, without which the blood, and therefore the life, cannot be nourished, is this oxygen. Now it is this very same air which the iron breathes when it gets rusty. It takes the oxygen from the atmosphere as eagerly as we do, though it uses it differently. The iron keeps all that it gets; we, and other animals, part with it again; but the metal absolutely keeps what it has once received of this aerial gift; and the ochreous dust which we so much despise is, in fact, just so much nobler than pure iron, in so far as it is *iron and the air*. Nobler, and more useful—for, indeed, as I shall be able to show you presently—the main service of this metal, and of all other metals, to us, is not in making knives, and scissors, and pokers, and pans, but in making the ground we feed from, and nearly all the substances first needful to our existence. For these are all nothing but metals and oxygen—metals with breath put into them. Sand, lime, clay, and the rest of the earths—potash and soda, and the rest of the alkalies—are all of them metals which have undergone this, so to speak, vital change, and have been rendered fit for the service of man by permanent unity with the purest air which he himself breathes. There is only one metal which does not rust readily; and that, in its influence on Man hitherto, has caused Death rather than Life; it will not be put to its right use till it is made a pavement of, and so trodden under foot.

Is there not something striking in this fact, considered largely as one of the types, or lessons, furnished by the inanimate creation? Here you have your hard, bright, cold, lifeless metal—good enough for swords and scissors—but not for food. You think, perhaps, that your iron is wonderfully useful in a pure form, but how would you like the world, if all your meadows, instead of grass, grew nothing but iron wire—if all your arable ground, instead of being made of sand and clay, were suddenly turned into flat surfaces of steel—if the whole earth, instead of its green and glowing sphere, rich with forest and flower, showed nothing but the image of the vast furnace of a ghastly engine—a globe of black, lifeless, excoriated metal? It would be that,—probably it was once that; but assuredly it would be, were it not that all the substance of which it is made sucks and breathes the brilliancy of the atmosphere; and as it breathes, softening from its merciless hardness, it falls into fruitful and beneficent dust; gathering itself again into the earths from which we feed, and the stones with which we build;— into the rocks that frame the mountains, and the sands that bind the sea.

Hence, it is impossible for you to take up the most insignificant pebble at your feet, without being able to read, if you like, this curious lesson in it. You look upon it at first as if it were earth only. Nay, it answers, "I am not earth—I am earth and air in one; part of that blue heaven which you love, and long for, is already in me; it is all my life—without it I should be nothing, and able for nothing; I could not minister to you, nor nourish you—I should be a cruel and helpless thing; but, because there is, according to my need and place in creation, a kind of soul in me, I have become capable of good, and helpful in the circles of vitality."

Thus far the same interest attaches to all the earths, and all the metals of which they are made; but a deeper interest, and larger beneficence belong to that ochreous earth of iron which stains the marble of your springs. It stains much besides that marble. It stains the great earth wheresoever you can see it, far and wide—it is the colouring substance appointed to colour the globe for the sight, as well as subdue it to the service of man. You have just seen your hills covered with snow, and, perhaps, have enjoyed, at first, the contrast of their fair white with the dark blocks of pine woods; but have you ever considered how you would like them always white—not pure white, but dirty white—the white of thaw, with all the chill of snow in it, but none of its brightness? That is what the colour of the earth would be without its iron; that would be its colour, not here or there only, but in all places, and at all times. Follow out that idea till you get it in some detail. Think first of your pretty gravel walks in your gardens, yellow and fine, like plots of sunshine between the flower-beds; fancy them all suddenly turned to the colour of ashes. That is what they would be without iron ochre. Think of your winding walks over the common, as warm to the eye as they are dry to the foot, and imagine them all laid down suddenly with gray cinders. Then pass beyond the common into the country, and pause at the first ploughed field that you see sweeping up the hill sides in the sun, with its deep brown furrows, and wealth of ridges all a-glow, heaved aside by the ploughshare, like deep folds of a mantle of russet velvet—fancy it all changed suddenly into grisly furrows in a field of mud. That is what it would be without iron. Pass on, in fancy, over hill and dale, till you reach the bending line of the sea shore; go down upon its breezy beach—watch the white foam flashing among the amber of it, and all the blue sea embayed in belts of gold: then fancy those circlets of far sweeping shore suddenly put into mounds of mourning—all those golden sands turned into gray slime, the fairies no more able to call to each other, "Come unto these yellow sands;" but, "Come unto these drab sands." That is what they would be, without iron.

Iron is in some sort, therefore, the sunshine and light of landscape, so far as that light depends on the ground; but it is a source of another kind of sunshine, quite as important to us in the way we live at present—sunshine, not of landscape, but of dwelling-place.

In these days of swift locomotion I may doubtless assume that most of my audience have been somewhere out of England—have been in Scotland, or France, or Switzerland. Whatever may have been their impression, on returning to their own country, of its superiority or inferiority in other respects, they cannot but have felt one thing about it—the comfortable look of its towns and villages. Foreign towns are often very picturesque, very beautiful, but they never have quite that look of warm self-sufficiency and wholesome quiet, with which our villages nestle themselves down among the green fields. If you will take the trouble to examine into the sources of this impression, you will find that by far the greater part of that warm and satisfactory appearance depends upon the rich scarlet colour of the bricks and tiles. It does not belong to the neat building— very neat building has an uncomfortable rather than a comfortable look—but it depends on the *warm* building; our villages are dressed in red tiles as our old women are in red cloaks; and it does not matter how worn the cloaks, or how bent and bowed the roof may be, so long as there are no holes in either one or the other, and the sobered but unextinguishable colour still glows in the shadow of the hood, and burns among the green mosses of the gable. And what do you suppose dyes your tiles of cottage roof? You don't paint them. It is nature who puts all that lovely vermilion into the clay for you; and all that lovely vermilion is this oxide of iron. Think, therefore, what your streets of towns would become—ugly enough, indeed, already, some of them, but still comfortable-looking— if instead of that warm brick red, the houses became all pepper-and- salt colour. Fancy your country villages changing from that homely scarlet of theirs which, in its sweet suggestion of laborious peace, is as honourable as the soldiers' scarlet of laborious battle—suppose all those cottage roofs, I say, turned at once into the colour of unbaked clay, the colour of street gutters in rainy weather. That's what they would be, without iron.

There is, however, yet another effect of colour in our English country towns which, perhaps, you may not all yourselves have noticed, but for which you must take the word of a sketcher. They are not so often merely warm scarlet as they are warm purple;—a more beautiful colour still: and they owe this colour to a mingling with the vermilion of the deep grayish or purple hue of our fine Welsh slates on the more respectable roofs, made more blue still by the colour of intervening atmosphere. If you examine one of these Welsh slates freshly broken, you will find its purple colour clear and vivid; and although never strikingly so after it has been long exposed to weather, it always retains enough of the tint to give rich harmonies of distant purple in opposition to the green of our woods and fields. Whatever brightness or power there is in the hue is entirely owing to the oxide of iron. Without it the slates would either be pale stone colour, or cold gray, or black.

Thus far we have only been considering the use and pleasantness of iron in the common earth of clay. But there are three kinds of earth which in mixed mass and prevalent quantity, form the world. Those are, in common language, the earths of clay, of lime, and of flint. Many other elements are mingled with these in sparing quantities; but the great frame and substance of the earth is made of these three, so that wherever you stand on solid ground, in any country of the globe, the thing that is mainly under your feet will be either clay, limestone, or some condition of the earth of flint, mingled with both.

These being what we have usually to deal with, Nature seems to have set herself to make these three substances as interesting to us, and as beautiful for us, as she can. The clay, being a soft and changeable substance, she doesn't take much pains about, as we have seen, till it is baked; she brings the colour into it only when it receives a permanent form. But the limestone and flint she paints, in her own way, in their native state: and her object in painting them seems to be much the same as in her painting of flowers; to draw us, careless and idle human creatures, to watch her a little, and see what she is about—that being on the whole good for us,—her children. For Nature is always carrying on very strange work with this limestone and flint of hers: laying down beds of them at the bottom of the sea; building islands out of the sea; filling chinks and veins in mountains with curious treasures; petrifying mosses, and trees, and shells; in fact, carrying on all sorts of business, subterranean or submarine, which it would be highly desirable for us, who profit and live by it, to notice as it goes on. And apparently to lead us to do this, she makes picture-books for us of limestone and flint; and tempts us, like foolish children as we are, to read her books by the pretty colours in them. The pretty colours in her limestone-books form those variegated marbles which all mankind have taken delight to polish and build with from the beginning of time; and the pretty colours in her flint-books form those agates, jaspers, cornelians, bloodstones, onyxes, cairngorms, chrysoprases, which men have in like manner taken delight to cut, and polish, and make ornaments of, from the beginning of time; and yet, so much of babies are they, and so fond of looking at the pictures instead of reading the book, that I question whether, after six thousand years of cutting and polishing, there are above two or three people out of any given hundred, who know, or care to know, how a bit of agate or a bit of marble was made, or painted.

How it was made, may not be always very easy to say; but with what it was painted there is no manner of question. All those beautiful violet veinings and variegations of the marbles of Sicily and Spain, the glowing orange and amber colours of those of Siena, the deep russet of the Rosso antico, and the blood-colour of all the precious jaspers that enrich the temples of Italy; and, finally, all the lovely transitions of tint in the pebbles of Scotland and the Rhine, which form, though not the most precious, by far the most interesting portion of our modern jewellers' work;—all these are painted by nature with this one material only, variously proportioned and applied—the oxide of iron that stains your Tunbridge springs.

But this is not all, nor the best part of the work of iron. Its service in producing these beautiful stones is only rendered to rich people, who can afford to quarry and polish them. But Nature paints for all the world, poor and rich together: and while, therefore, she thus adorns the innermost rocks of her hills, to tempt your investigation, or indulge your luxury,—she paints, far more carefully, the outsides of the hills, which are for the eyes of the shepherd and the ploughman. I spoke just now of the effect in the roofs of our villages of their purple slates: but if the slates are beautiful even in their flat and formal rows on house-roofs, much more are they beautiful on the rugged crests and flanks of their native mountains. Have you ever considered, in speaking as we do so often of distant blue hills, what it is that makes them blue? To a certain extent it is distance; but distance alone will not do it. Many hills look white, however distant. That lovely dark purple colour of our Welsh and Highland hills is owing, not to their distance merely, but to their rocks. Some of their rocks are, indeed, too dark to be beautiful, being black or ashy gray; owing to imperfect and porous structure. But when you see this dark colour dashed with russet and blue, and coming out in masses among the green ferns, so purple that you can hardly tell at first whether it is rock or heather, then you must thank your old Tunbridge friend, the oxide of iron.

But this is not all. It is necessary for the beauty of hill scenery that Nature should colour not only her soft rocks, but her hard ones; and she colours them with the same thing, only more beautifully. Perhaps you have wondered at my use of the word "purple," so often of stones; but the Greeks, and still more the Romans, who had profound respect for purple, used it of stone long ago. You have all heard of "porphyry" as among the most precious of the harder massive stones. The colour which gave it that noble name, as well as that which gives the flush to all the rosy granite of Egypt—yes, and to the rosiest summits of the Alps themselves—is still owing to the same substance—your humble oxide of iron.

And last of all:

A nobler colour than all these—the noblest colour ever seen on this earth—one which belongs to a strength greater than that of the Egyptian granite, and to a beauty greater than that of the sunset or the rose—is still mysteriously connected with the presence of this dark iron. I believe it is not ascertained on what the crimson of blood actually depends; but the colour is connected, of course, with its vitality, and that vitality with the existence of iron as one of its substantial elements.

Is it not strange to find this stern and strong metal mingled so delicately in our human life, that we cannot even blush without its help? Think of it, my fair and gentle hearers; how terrible the alternative—sometimes you have actually no choice but to be brazen-faced, or iron-faced!

In this slight review of some of the functions of the metal, you observe that I confine myself strictly to its operations as a colouring element. I should only confuse your conception of the facts, if I endeavoured to describe its uses as a substantial element, either in strengthening rocks, or influencing vegetation by the decomposition of rocks. I have not, therefore, even glanced at any of the more serious uses of the metal in the economy of nature. But what I wish you to carry clearly away with you is the remembrance that in all these uses the metal would be nothing without the air. The pure metal has no power, and never occurs in nature at all except in meteoric stones, whose fall no one can account for, and which are useless after they have fallen: in the necessary work of the world, the iron is invariably joined with the oxygen, and would be capable of no service or beauty whatever without it.

II. IRON IN ART.—Passing, then, from the offices of the metal in the operations of nature to its uses in the hands of man, you must remember, in the outset, that the type which has been thus given you, by the lifeless metal, of the action of body and soul together, has noble antitype in the operation of all human power. All art worthy the name is the energy—neither of the human body alone, nor of the human soul alone, but of both united, one guiding the other: good craftsmanship and work of the fingers, joined with good emotion and work of the heart.

There is no good art, nor possible judgment of art, when these two are not united; yet we are constantly trying to separate them. Our amateurs cannot be persuaded but that they may produce some kind of art by their fancy or sensibility, without going through the necessary manual toil. That is entirely hopeless. Without a certain number, and that a very great number, of steady acts of hand—a practice as careful and constant as would be necessary to learn any other manual business—no drawing is possible. On the other side, the workman, and those who employ him, are continually trying to produce art by trick or habit of fingers, without using their fancy or sensibility. That also is hopeless. Without mingling of heart-passion with hand-power, no art is possible. [Footnote: No fine art, that is. See the previous definition of fine art at p. 38.] The highest art unites both in their intensest degrees: the action of the hand at its finest, with that of the heart at its fullest.

Hence it follows that the utmost power of art can only be given in a material capable of receiving and retaining the influence of the subtlest touch of the human hand. That hand is the most perfect agent of material power existing in the universe; and its full subtlety can only be shown when the material it works on, or with, is entirely yielding. The chords of a perfect instrument will receive it, but not of an imperfect one; the softly bending point of the hair pencil, and soft melting of colour, will receive it, but not even the chalk or pen point, still less the steel point, chisel, or marble. The hand of a sculptor may, indeed, be as subtle as that of a painter, but all its subtlety is not bestowable nor expressible: the touch of Titian, Correggio, or Turner, [Footnote: See Appendix IV., "Subtlety of Hand."] is a far more marvellous piece of nervous action than can be shown in anything but colour, or in the very highest conditions of executive expression in music. In proportion as the material worked upon is less delicate, the execution necessarily becomes lower, and the art with it. This is one main principle of all work. Another is, that whatever the material you choose to work with, your art is base if it does not bring out the distinctive qualities of that material.

The reason of this second law is, that if you don't want the qualities of the substance you use, you ought to use some other substance: it can be only affectation, and desire to display your skill, that lead you to employ a refractory substance, and therefore your art will all be base. Glass, for instance, is eminently, in its nature, transparent. If you don't want transparency, let the glass alone. Do not try to make a window look like an opaque picture, but take an opaque ground to begin with. Again, marble is eminently a solid and massive substance. Unless you want mass and solidity, don't work in marble. If you wish for lightness, take wood; if for freedom, take stucco; if for ductility, take glass. Don't try to carve leathers, or trees, or nets, or foam, out of marble. Carve white limbs and broad breasts only out of that.

So again, iron is eminently a ductile and tenacious substance— tenacious above all things, ductile more than most. When you want tenacity, therefore, and involved form, take iron. It is eminently made for that. It is the material given to the sculptor as the companion of marble, with a message, as plain as it can well be spoken, from the lips of the earth-mother, "Here's for you to cut, and here's for you to hammer. Shape this, and twist that. What is solid and simple, carve out; what is thin and entangled, beat out. I give you all kinds of forms to be delighted in;—fluttering leaves as well as fair bodies; twisted branches as well as open brows. The leaf and the branch you may beat and drag into their imagery: the body and brow you shall reverently touch into their imagery. And if you choose rightly and work rightly, what you do shall be safe afterwards. Your slender leaves shall not break off in my tenacious iron, though they may be rusted a little with an iron autumn. Your broad surfaces shall not be unsmoothed in my pure crystalline marble—no decay shall touch them. But if you carve in the marble what will break with a touch, or mould in the metal what a stain of rust or verdigris will spoil, it is your fault—not mine."

These are the main principles in this matter; which, like nearly all other right principles in art, we moderns delight in contradicting as directly and specially as may be. We continually look for, and praise, in our exhibitions the sculpture of veils, and lace, and thin leaves, and all kinds of impossible things pushed as far as possible in the fragile stone, for the sake of showing the sculptor's dexterity. [Footnote: I do not mean to attach any degree of blame to the effort to represent leafage in marble for certain expressive purposes. The later works of Mr. Munro have depended for some of their most tender thoughts on a delicate and skilful use of such accessories. And in general, leaf sculpture is good and admirable, if it renders, as in Gothic work, the grace and lightness of the leaf by the arrangement of light and shadow —supporting the masses well by strength of stone below; but all carving is base which proposes to itself *slightness* as an aim, and tries to imitate the absolute thinness of thin or slight things, as much modern wood carving does, I saw in Italy, a year or two ago, a marble sculpture of birds› nests.] On the other hand, we *cast* our iron into bars—brittle, though an inch thick—sharpen them at the ends, and consider fences, and other work, made of such materials, decorative! I do not believe it would be easy to calculate the amount of mischief done to our taste in England by that fence iron-work of ours alone. If it were asked of us by a single characteristic, to distinguish the dwellings of a country into two broad sections; and to set, on one side, the places where people were, for the most part, simple, happy, benevolent, and honest; and, on the other side, the places where at least a great number of the people were sophisticated, unkind, uncomfortable, and unprincipled, there is, I think, one feature that you could fix upon as a positive test: the uncomfortable and unprincipled parts of a country would be the parts where people lived among iron railings, and the comfortable and principled parts where they had none. A broad generalization, you will say! Perhaps a little too broad; yet, in all sobriety, it will come truer than you think. Consider every other kind of fence or defence, and you will find some virtue in it; but in the iron railing none. There is, first, your castle rampart of stone—somewhat too grand to be considered here among our types of fencing; next, your garden or park wall of brick, which has indeed often an unkind look on the outside, but there is more modesty in it than unkindness. It generally means, not that the builder of it wants to shut you out from the view of his garden, but from the view of himself: it is a frank statement that as he needs a certain portion of time to himself, so he needs a certain portion of ground to himself, and must not be stared at when he digs there in his shirt- sleeves, or plays at leapfrog with his boys from school, or talks over old times with his wife, walking up and down in the evening sunshine. Besides, the brick wall has good practical service in it, and shelters you from the east wind, and ripens your peaches and nectarines, and glows in autumn like a sunny bank. And, moreover, your brick wall, if you build it properly, so that it shall stand long enough, is a beautiful thing when it is old, and has assumed its grave purple red, touched with mossy green.

Next to your lordly wall, in dignity of enclosure, comes your close-set wooden paling, which is more objectionable, because it commonly means enclosure on a larger scale than people want. Still it is significative of pleasant parks, and well-kept field walks, and herds of deer, and other such aristocratic pastoralisms, which have here and there their proper place in a country, and may be passed without any discredit.

Next to your paling, comes your low stone dyke, your mountain fence, indicative at a glance either of wild hill country, or of beds of stone beneath the soil; the hedge of the mountains—delightful in all its associations, and yet more in the varied and craggy forms of the loose stones it is built of; and next to the low stone wall, your lowland hedge, either in trim line of massive green, suggested of the pleasances of old Elizabethan houses, and smooth alleys for aged feet, and quaint labyrinths for young ones, or else in fair entanglement of eglantine and virgin's bower, tossing its scented luxuriance along our country waysides;—how many such you have here among your pretty hills, fruitful with black clusters of the bramble for boys in autumn, and crimson hawthorn berries for birds in winter. And then last, and most difficult to class among fences, comes your handrail, expressive of all sorts of things; sometimes having a knowing and vicious look, which it learns at race-courses; sometimes an innocent and tender look, which it learns at rustic bridges over cressy brooks; and sometimes a prudent and protective look, which it learns on passes of the Alps, where it has posts of granite and bars of pine, and guards the brows of cliffs and the banks of torrents. So that in all these kinds of defence there is some good, pleasant, or noble meaning. But what meaning has the iron railing? Either, observe, that you are living in the midst of such bad characters that you must keep them out by main force of bar, or that you are yourself of a character requiring to be kept inside in the same manner. Your iron railing always means thieves outside, or Bedlam inside; it *can* mean nothing else than that. If the people outside were good for anything, a hint in the way of fence would be enough for them; but because they are violent and at enmity with you, you are forced to put the close bars and the spikes at the top.

Last summer I was lodging for a little while in a cottage in the country, and in front of my low window there were, first some beds of daisies, then a row of gooseberry and currant bushes, and then a low wall about three feet above the ground, covered with stone-cress. Outside, a corn-field, with its green ears glistening in the sun, and a field path through it, just past the garden gate. From my window I could see every peasant of the village who passed that way, with basket on arm for market, or spade on shoulder for field. When I was inclined for society, I could lean over my wall, and talk to anybody; when I was inclined for science, I could botanize all along the top of my wall— there were four species of stone-cress alone growing on it; and when I was inclined for exercise, I could jump over my wall, backwards and forwards. That's the sort of fence to have in a Christian country; not a thing which you can't walk inside of without making yourself look like a wild beast, nor look at out of your window in the morning without expecting to see somebody impaled upon it in the night.

And yet farther, observe that the iron railing is a useless fence—it can shelter nothing, and support nothing; you can't nail your peaches to it, nor protect your flowers with it, nor make anything whatever out of its costly tyranny; and besides being useless, it is an insolent fence;—it says plainly to everybody who passes—"You may be an honest person,—but, also, you may be a thief: honest or not, you shall not get in here, for I am a respectable person, and much above you;

you shall only see what a grand place I have got to keep you out of—
look here, and depart in humiliation."

This, however, being in the present state of civilization a frequent
manner of discourse, and there being unfortunately many districts
where the iron railing is unavoidable, it yet remains a question
whether you need absolutely make it ugly, no less than significative
of evil. You must have railings round your squares in London, and at
the sides of your areas; but need you therefore have railings so ugly
that the constant sight of them is enough to neutralise the effect of
all the schools of art in the kingdom? You need not. Far from such
necessity, it is even in your power to turn all your police force of iron
bars actually into drawing masters, and natural historians. Not, of
course, without some trouble and some expense; you can do nothing
much worth doing, in this world, without trouble, you can get nothing
much worth having without expense. The main question is only—
what is worth doing and having:—Consider, therefore, if this be not.
Here is your iron railing, as yet, an uneducated monster; a sombre
seneschal, incapable of any words, except his perpetual "Keep out!"
and "Away with you!" Would it not be worth some trouble and cost
to turn this ungainly ruffian porter into a well-educated servant; who,
while he was severe as ever in forbidding entrance to evilly-disposed
people, should yet have a kind word for well-disposed people, and a
pleasant look, and a little useful information at his command, in case
he should be asked a question by the passers-by?

We have not time to-night to look at many examples of ironwork;
and those I happen to have by me are not the best; ironwork is not one
of my special subjects of study; so that I only have memoranda of bits
that happened to come into picturesque subjects which I was drawing
for other reasons. Besides, external ironwork is more difficult to find
good than any other sort of ancient art; for when it gets rusty and
broken, people are sure, if they can afford it, to send it to the old iron
shop, and get a fine new grating instead; and in the great cities of
Italy, the old iron is thus nearly all gone: the best bits I remember in
the open air were at Brescia;—fantastic sprays of laurel- like foliage
rising over the garden gates; and there are a few fine fragments at
Verona, and some good trellis-work enclosing the Scala tombs; but
on the whole, the most interesting pieces, though by no means the
purest in style, are to be found in out-of-the-way provincial towns,

where people do not care, or are unable, to make polite alterations. The little town of Bellinzona, for instance, on the south of the Alps, and that of Sion on the north, have both of them complete schools of ironwork in their balconies and vineyard gates. That of Bellinzona is the best, though not very old—I suppose most of it of the seventeenth century; still it is very quaint and beautiful. Here, for example, are two balconies, from two different houses; one has been a cardinal's, and the hat is the principal ornament of the balcony; its tassels being wrought with delightful delicacy and freedom; and catching the eye clearly even among the mass of rich wreathed leaves. These tassels and strings are precisely the kind of subject fit for ironwork—noble in ironwork, they would have been entirely ignoble in marble, on the grounds above stated. The real plant of oleander standing in the window enriches the whole group of lines very happily.

The other balcony, from a very ordinary-looking house in the same street, is much more interesting in its details. It is shown in the plate as it appeared last summer, with convolvulus twined about the bars, the arrow-shaped living leaves mingled among the leaves of iron; but you may see in the centre of these real leaves a cluster of lighter ones, which are those of the ironwork itself. This cluster is worth giving a little larger to show its treatment. Fig. 2 (in Appendix V.) is the front view of it: Fig. 4, its profile. It is composed of a large tulip in the centre; then two turkscap lilies; then two pinks, a little conventionalized; then two narcissi; then two nondescripts, or, at least, flowers I do not know; and then two dark buds, and a few leaves. I say, dark buds, for all these flowers have been coloured in their original state. The plan of the group is exceedingly simple: it is all enclosed in a pointed arch (Fig. 3, Appendix V.): the large mass of the tulip forming the apex; a six-foiled star on each side; then a jagged star; then a five-foiled star; then an unjagged star or rose; finally a small bud, so as to establish relation and cadence through the whole group. The profile is very free and fine, and the upper bar of the balcony exceedingly beautiful in effect;—none the less so on account of the marvellously simple means employed. A thin strip of iron is bent over a square rod; out of the edge of this strip are cut a series of triangular openings—widest at top, leaving projecting teeth of iron (Appendix, Fig. 5); then each of these projecting pieces gets a little sharp tap with the hammer in front, which beaks its edge inwards, tearing it a little open at the same time, and the thing is done.

The common forms of Swiss ironwork are less naturalistic than these Italian balconies, depending more on beautiful arrangements of various curve; nevertheless, there has been a rich naturalist school at Fribourg, where a few bell-handles are still left, consisting of rods branched into laurel and other leafage. At Geneva, modern improvements have left nothing; but at Annecy, a little good work remains; the balcony of its old hôtel de ville especially, with a trout of the lake —presumably the town arms—forming its central ornament.

I might expatiate all night—if you would sit and hear me—on the treatment of such required subject, or introduction of pleasant caprice by the old workmen; but we have no more time to spare, and I must quit this part of our subject—the rather as I could not explain to you the intrinsic merit of such ironwork without going fully into the theory of curvilinear design; only let me leave with you this one distinct assertion—that the quaint beauty and character of many natural objects, such as intricate branches, grass, foliage (especially thorny branches and prickly foliage), as well as that of many animals, plumed, spined, or bristled, is sculpturally expressible in iron only, and in iron would be majestic and impressive in the highest degree; and that every piece of metal work you use might be, rightly treated, not only a superb decoration, but a most valuable abstract of portions of natural forms, holding in dignity precisely the same relation to the painted representation of plants, that a statue does to the painted form of man. It is difficult to give you an idea of the grace and interest which the simplest objects possess when their forms are thus abstracted from among the surrounding of rich circumstance which in nature disturbs the feebleness of our attention. In Plate 2, a few blades of common green grass, and a wild leaf or two—just as they were thrown by nature,—are thus abstracted from the associated redundance of the forms about them, and shown on a dark ground: every cluster of herbage would furnish fifty such groups, and every such group would work into iron (fitting it, of course, rightly to its service) with perfect ease, and endless grandeur of result.

III. IRON in POLICY.—Having thus obtained some idea of the use of iron in art, as dependent on its ductility, I need not, certainly, say anything of its uses in manufacture and commerce; we all of us know enough,—perhaps a little too much—about *them*. So I pass lastly to consider its uses in policy; dependent chiefly upon its tenacity— that is to say, on its power of bearing a pull, and receiving an edge. These powers, which enable it to pierce, to bind, and to smite, render it fit for the three great instruments, by which its political action may be simply typified; namely, the Plough, the Fetter, and the Sword.

On our understanding the right use of these three instruments, depend, of course, all our power as a nation, and all our happiness as individuals.

I. THE PLOUGH.—I say, first, on our understanding the right use of the plough, with which, in justice to the fairest of our labourers, we must always associate that feminine plough—the needle. The first requirement for the happiness of a nation is that it should understand the function in this world of these two great instruments: a happy nation may be defined as one in which the husband's hand is on the plough, and the housewife's on the needle; so in due time reaping its golden harvest, and shining in golden vesture: and an unhappy nation is one which, acknowledging no use of plough nor needle, will assuredly at last find its storehouse empty in the famine, and its breast naked to the cold.

Perhaps you think this is a mere truism, which I am wasting your time in repeating. I wish it were.

By far the greater part of the suffering and crime which exist at this moment in civilized Europe, arises simply from people not understanding this truism—not knowing that produce or wealth is eternally connected by the laws of heaven and earth with resolute labour; but hoping in some way to cheat or abrogate this everlasting law of life, and to feed where they have not furrowed, and be warm where they have not woven.

I repeat, nearly all our misery and crime result from this one misapprehension. The law of nature is, that a certain quantity of work is necessary to produce a certain quantity of good, of any kind whatever. If you want knowledge, you must toil for it: if food, you must toil for it; and if pleasure, you must toil for it. But men do not acknowledge this law, or strive to evade it, hoping to get their knowledge, and food, and pleasure for nothing; and in this effort they either fail of getting them, and remain ignorant and miserable, or they obtain them by making other men work for their benefit; and then they are tyrants and robbers. Yes, and worse than robbers. I am not one who in the least doubts or disputes the progress of this century in many things useful to mankind; but it seems to me a very dark sign respecting us that we look with so much indifference upon dishonesty and cruelty in the pursuit of wealth. In the dream of Nebuchadnezzar it was only the *feet* that were part of iron and part of clay; but many of us are now getting so cruel in our avarice, that it seems as if, in us, the *heart* were part of iron, and part of clay.

From what I have heard of the inhabitants of this town, I do not doubt but that I may be permitted to do here what I have found it usually thought elsewhere highly improper and absurd to do, namely, trace a few Bible sentences to their practical result.

You cannot but have noticed how often in those parts of the Bible which are likely to be oftenest opened when people look for guidance, comfort, or help in the affairs of daily life, namely, the Psalms and Proverbs, mention is made of the guilt attaching to the *Oppression* of the poor. Observe: not the neglect of them, but the *Oppression* of them: the word is as frequent as it is strange. You can hardly open either of those books, but somewhere in their pages you will find a description of the wicked man›s attempts against the poor: such as—"He doth ravish the poor when he getteth him into his net."

"He sitteth in the lurking places of the villages; his eyes are privily set against the poor."

"In his pride he doth persecute the poor, and blesseth the covetous, whom God abhorreth."

"His mouth is full of deceit and fraud; in the secret places doth he murder the innocent. Have the workers of iniquity no knowledge, who eat up my people as they eat bread? They have drawn out the sword, and bent the bow, to cast down the poor and needy."

"They are corrupt, and speak wickedly concerning oppression."

"Pride compasseth them about as a chain, and violence as a garment."

"Their poison is like the poison of a serpent. Ye weigh the violence of your hands in the earth."

Yes: "Ye weigh the violence of your hands:"—weigh these words as well. The last things we ever usually think of weighing are Bible words. We like to dream and dispute over them; but to weigh them, and see what their true contents are—anything but that. Yet, weigh these; for I have purposely taken all these verses, perhaps more striking to you read in this connection, than separately in their places, out of the Psalms, because, for all people belonging to the Established Church of this country these Psalms are appointed lessons, portioned out to them by their clergy to be read once through every month. Presumably, therefore, whatever portions of Scripture we may pass by or forget, these at all events, must be brought continually to our observance as useful for direction of daily life. Now, do we ever ask ourselves what the real meaning of these passages may be, and who these wicked people are, who are "murdering the innocent?" You know it is rather singular language this!—rather strong language, we might, perhaps, call it— hearing it for the first time. Murder! and murder of innocent people!— nay, even a sort of cannibalism. Eating people,—yes, and God's people, too—eating *My* people as if they were bread! swords drawn, bows bent, poison of serpents mixed! violence of hands weighed, measured, and trafficked with as so much coin! where is all this going on? Do you suppose it was only going on in the time of David, and that nobody but Jews ever murder the poor? If so, it would surely be wiser not to mutter and mumble for our daily lessons what does not concern us; but if there be any chance that it may concern us, and if this description, in the Psalms, of human guilt is at all generally applicable, as the descriptions in the Psalms of human sorrow are, may it not be advisable to know wherein this guilt is being committed round about us, or by ourselves? and when we take the words of the Bible into our mouths in a congregational way, to be sure whether we mean merely to chant a piece of melodious poetry relating to other people—(we know not exactly to whom)—or to assert our belief in facts bearing somewhat stringently on ourselves and our daily business. And if you make up your minds to do this no longer, and take pains to examine into the matter, you will find that these strange words, occurring as they do, not in a few places only, but almost in every alternate psalm and every alternate chapter of proverb, or prophecy, with tremendous reiteration, were not written for one nation or one time only; but for all nations and languages, for all places and all centuries; and it is as true of the wicked man now as ever it was of Nabal or Dives, that "his eyes are set against the poor."

Set *against* the poor, mind you. Not merely set *away* from the poor, so as to neglect or lose sight of them, but set against, so as to afflict and destroy them. This is the main point I want to fix. your attention upon. You will often hear sermons about neglect or carelessness of the poor. But neglect and carelessness are not at all the points. The Bible hardly ever talks about neglect of the poor. It always talks of *oppression* of the poor—a very different matter. It does not merely speak of passing by on the other side, and binding up no wounds, but of drawing the sword and ourselves smiting the men down. It does not charge us with being idle in the pest-house, and giving no medicine, but with being busy in the pest-house, and giving much poison.

May we not advisedly look into this matter a little, even tonight, and ask first, Who are these poor?

No country is, or ever will be, without them: that is to say, without the class which cannot, on the average, do more by its labour than provide for its subsistence, and which has no accumulations of property laid by on any considerable scale. Now there are a certain number of this class whom we cannot oppress with much severity. An able-bodied and intelligent workman—sober, honest, and industrious, will almost always command a fair price for his work, and lay by enough in a few years to enable him to hold his own in the labour market. But all men are not able-bodied, nor intelligent, nor industrious; and you cannot expect them to be. Nothing appears to me at once more ludicrous and more melancholy than the way the people of the present age usually talk about the morals of labourers. You hardly ever address a labouring man upon his prospects in life, without quietly assuming that he is to possess, at starting, as a small moral capital to begin with, the virtue of Socrates, the philosophy of Plato, and the heroism of Epaminondas. "Be assured, my good man,"—you say to him,—"that if you work steadily for ten hours a day all your life long, and if you drink nothing but water, or the very mildest beer, and live on very plain food, and never lose your temper, and go to church every Sunday, and always remain content in the position in which Providence has placed you, and never grumble nor swear; and always keep your clothes decent, and rise early, and use every opportunity of improving yourself, you will get on very well, and never come to the parish."

All this is exceedingly true; but before giving the advice so confidently, it would be well if we sometimes tried it practically ourselves, and spent a year or so at some hard manual labour, not of an entertaining kind—ploughing or digging, for instance, with a very moderate allowance of beer; nothing hut bread and cheese for dinner; no papers nor muffins in the morning; no sofas nor magazines at night; one small room for parlour and kitchen; and a large family of children always in the middle of the floor. If we think we could, under these circumstances, enact Socrates or Epaminondas entirely to our own satisfaction, we shall be somewhat justified in requiring the same behaviour from our poorer neighbours; but if not, we should surely consider a little whether among the various forms of the oppression of the poor, we may not rank as one of the first and likeliest—the oppression of expecting too much from them.

But let this pass; and let it be admitted that we can never be guilty of oppression towards the sober, industrious, intelligent, exemplary labourer. There will always be in the world some who are not altogether, intelligent and exemplary; we shall, I believe, to the end of time find the majority somewhat unintelligent, a little inclined to be idle, and occasionally, on Saturday night, drunk; we must even be prepared to hear of reprobates who like skittles on Sunday morning better than prayers; and of unnatural parents who send their children out to beg instead of to go to school.

Now these are the kind of people whom you *can* oppress, and whom you do oppress, and that to purpose,—and with all the more cruelty and the greater sting, because it is just their own fault that puts them into your power. You know the words about wicked people are, "He doth ravish the poor when he getteth him *into his net*." This getting into the net is constantly the fault or folly of the sufferer—his own heedlessness or his own indolence; but after he is once in the net, the oppression of him, and making the most of his distress, are ours. The nets which we use against the poor are just those worldly embarrassments which either their ignorance or their improvidence are almost certain at some time or other to bring them into: then, just at the time when we ought to hasten to help them, and disentangle them, and teach them how to manage better in future, we rush forward to *pillage* them, and force all we can out of them in their adversity. For, to take one instance only, remember this is literally and simply what we do, whenever we buy, or try to buy, cheap goods— goods offered at a price which we know cannot be remunerative for the labour involved in them. Whenever we buy such goods, remember we are stealing somebody's labour. Don't let us mince the matter. I say, in plain Saxon, STEALING—taking from him the proper reward of his work, and putting it into our own pocket. You know well enough that the thing could not have been offered you at that price, unless distress of some kind had forced the producer to part with it. You take advantage of this distress, and you force as much out of him as you can under the circumstances. The old barons of the middle ages used, in general, the thumbscrew to extort property; we moderns use, in preference, hunger or domestic affliction: but the fact of extortion remains precisely the same. Whether we force the man's property from him by pinching his stomach, or pinching his fingers, makes some difference anatomically;— morally, none whatsoever: we use a form of torture of some sort in order to make him give up his property; we use, indeed, the man's own anxieties, instead of the rack; and his immediate peril of starvation, instead of the pistol at the head; but otherwise we differ from Front de Buf, or Dick Turpin, merely in being less dexterous, more cowardly, and more cruel. More cruel, I say, because the fierce baron and the redoubted highwayman are reported to have robbed, at least by preference, only the rich; *we* steal habitually from the poor. We buy our liveries, and gild our prayer-books, with pilfered pence out of children's and sick men's wages, and thus ingeniously dispose a given quantity of Theft, so that it may produce the largest possible measure of delicately distributed suffering.

But this is only one form of common oppression of the poor— only one way of taking our hands off the plough handle, and binding another's upon it. This first way of doing it is the economical way— the way preferred by prudent and virtuous people. The bolder way is the acquisitive way:—the way of speculation. You know we are considering at present the various modes in which a nation corrupts itself, by not acknowledging the eternal connection between its plough and its pleasure;—by striving to get pleasure, without working for it. Well, I say the first and commonest way of doing so is to try to get the product of other people's work, and enjoy it ourselves, by cheapening their labour in times of distress: then the second way is that grand one of watching the chances of the market;—the way of speculation. Of course there are some speculations that are fair and honest—speculations made with our own money, and which do not involve in their success the loss, by others, of what we gain. But generally modern speculation involves much risk to others, with chance of profit only to ourselves: even in its best conditions it is merely one of the forms of gambling or treasure hunting; it is either leaving the steady plough and the steady pilgrimage of life, to look for silver mines beside the way; or else it is the full stop beside the dice-tables in Vanity Fair —investing all the thoughts and passions of the soul in the fall of the cards, and choosing rather the wild accidents of idle fortune than the calm and accumulative rewards of toil. And this is destructive enough, at least to our peace and virtue. But is usually destructive of far more than *our* peace, or *our* virtue. Have you ever deliberately set yourselves to imagine and measure the suffering, the guilt, and the mortality caused necessarily by the failure of any large-dealing merchant, or largely-branched bank? Take it at the lowest possible supposition- count, at the fewest you choose, the families whose means of support have been involved in the catastrophe. Then, on the morning after the intelli- gence of ruin, let us go forth amongst them in earnest thought; let us use that imagination which we waste so often on fictitious sorrow, to measure the stern facts of that multitudinous distress; strike open the private doors of their chambers, and enter silently into the midst of the domestic misery; look upon the old men, who had reserved for their failing strength some remainder of rest in the evening-tide of life, cast helplessly back into its trouble and tumult; look upon the active strength of middle age suddenly blasted into incapacity—its hopes crushed, and its hardly earned rewards snatched away in the same instant—at once the heart withered, and the right arm snapped; look upon the piteous children, delicately nurtured, whose soft eyes, now large with wonder at their parents' grief, must soon be set in the dimness of famine; and, far more than all this, look forward to the length of sorrow beyond—to the hardest labour of life, now to be undergone either in all the severity of unexpected and inexperienced trial, or else, more bitter still, to be begun again, and endured for the second time, amidst the ruins of cherished hopes and the feebleness of advancing years, embittered by the continual sting and taunt of the inner feeling that it has all been brought about, not by the fair course of appointed circumstance, but by miserable chance and wanton treachery; and, last of all, look beyond this—to the shattered destinies of those who have faltered under the trial, and sunk past recovery to despair. And then consider whether the hand which has poured this poison into all the springs of life be one whit less guiltily red with human blood than that which literally pours the hemlock into the cup, or guides the dagger to the heart? We read with horror of the crimes of a Borgia or a Tophana; but there never lived Borgias such as live now in the midst of us. The cruel lady of Ferrara slew only in the strength of passion—she slew only a few, those who thwarted her purposes or who vexed her soul; she slew sharply and suddenly, embittering the fate of her victims with no foretastes of destruction, no prolongations of pain; and, finally and chiefly, she slew, not without remorse, nor without pity. But *we*, in no storm of passion—in no blindness of wrath,—we, in calm and clear and untempted selfishness, pour our poison—not for a few only, but for multitudes;—not for those who have wronged us, or resisted,—but for those who have trusted us and aided:—we, not with sudden gift of merciful and unconscious death, but with slow waste of hunger and weary rack of disappointment and despair;—we, last and chiefly, do our murdering, not with any pauses of pity or scorching of conscience, but in facile and forgetful calm of mind—and so, forsooth, read day by day, complacently, as if they meant any one else than ourselves, the words that forever describe the wicked: "The *poison of asps* is under their lips, and their *feet are swift to shed blood*."

You may indeed, perhaps, think there is some excuse for many in this matter, just because the sin is so unconscious; that the guilt is not so great when it is unapprehended, and that it is much more pardonable to slay heedlessly than purposefully. I believe no feeling can be more mistaken, and that in reality, and in the sight of heaven; the callous indifference which pursues its own interests at any cost of life, though it does not definitely adopt the purpose of sin, is a state of mind at once more heinous and more hopeless than the wildest aberrations of ungoverned passion. There may be, in the last case, some elements of good and of redemption still mingled in the character; but, in the other, few or none. There may be hope for the man who has slain his enemy in anger; hope even for the man who has betrayed his friend in fear; but what hope for him who trades in unregarded blood, and builds his fortune on unrepented treason?

But, however this may be, and wherever you may think yourselves bound in justice to impute the greater sin, be assured that the question is one of responsibilities only, not of facts. The definite result of all our modern haste to be rich is assuredly, and constantly, the murder of a certain number of persons by our hands every year. I have not time to go into the details of another—on the whole, the broadest and terriblest way in which we cause the destruction of the poor—namely, the way of luxury and waste, destroying, in improvidence, what might have been the support of thousands; [Footnote: The analysis of this error will be found completely carried out in my lectures on the political economy of art. And it is an error worth analyzing; for until it is finally trodden under foot, no healthy political, economical, or moral action is *possible* in any state. I do not say this impetuously or suddenly, for I have investigated this subject as deeply; and as long, as my own special subject of art; and the principles of political economy which I have stated in those lectures are as sure as the principles of Euclid. Foolish readers doubted their certainty, because I told them I had "never read any books on Political Economy" Did they suppose I had got my knowledge of art by reading books?] but if you follow out the subject for yourselves at home—and what I have endeavoured to lay before you to-night will only be useful to you if you do—you will find that wherever and whenever men are endeavouring to *make money hastily*, and to avoid the labour which Providence has appointed to be the only source of honourable profit;—and also wherever and whenever they permit themselves to *spend it luxuriously*, without reflecting how far they are misguiding the labour of others;—there and then, in either case, they are literally and infallibly causing, for their own benefit or their own pleasure, a certain annual number of human deaths; that, therefore, the choice given to every man born into this world is, simply, whether he will be a labourer, or an assassin; and that whosoever has not his hand on the Stilt of the plough, has it on the Hilt of the dagger.

It would also be quite vain for me to endeavour to follow out this evening the lines of thought which would be suggested by the other two great political uses of iron in the Fetter and the Sword: a few words only I must permit myself respecting both.

2. THE FETTER.—As the plough is the typical instrument of industry, so the fetter is the typical instrument of the restraint or

subjection necessary in a nation—either literally, for its evil-doers, or figuratively, in accepted laws, for its wise and good men. You have to choose between this figurative and literal use; for depend upon it, the more laws you accept, the fewer penalties you will have to endure, and the fewer punishments to enforce. For wise laws and just restraints are to a noble nation not chains, but chain mail—strength and defence, though something also of an incumbrance. And this necessity of restraint, remember, is just as honourable to man as the necessity of labour. You hear every day greater numbers of foolish people speaking about liberty, as if it were such an honourable thing: so far from being that, it is, on the whole, and in the broadest sense, dishonourable, and an attribute of the lower creatures. No human being, however great or powerful, was ever so free as a fish. There is always something that he must, or must not do; while the fish may do whatever he likes. All the kingdoms of the world put together are not half so large as the sea, and all the railroads and wheels that ever were, or will be, invented are not so easy as fins. You will find, on fairly thinking of it, that it is his Restraint which is honourable to man, not his Liberty; and, what is more, it is restraint which is honourable even in the lower animals. A butterfly is much more free than a bee; but you honour the bee more, just because it is subject to certain laws which fit it for orderly function in bee society And throughout the world, of the two abstract things, liberty and restraint, restraint is always the more honourable. It is true, indeed, that in these and all other matters you never can reason finally from the abstraction, for both liberty and restraint are good when they are nobly chosen, and both are bad when they are basely chosen; but of the two, I repeat, it is restraint which characterizes the higher creature, and betters the lower creature: and, from the ministering of the archangel to the labour of the insect,— from the poising of the planets to the gravitation of a grain of dust,— the power and glory of all creatures, and all matter, consist in their obedience, not in their freedom. The Sun has no liberty—a dead leaf has much. The dust of which you are formed has no liberty. Its liberty will come—with its corruption.

And, therefore, I say boldly, though it seems a strange thing to say in England, that as the first power of a nation consists in knowing how to guide the Plough, its second power consists in knowing how to wear the Fetter:—

3. THE SWORD.—And its third power, which perfects it as a nation, consist in knowing how to wield the sword, so that the three talismans of national existence are expressed in these three short words—Labour, Law, and Courage.

This last virtue we at least possess; and all that is to be alleged against us is that we do not honour it enough. I do not mean honour by acknowledgment of service, though sometimes we are slow in doing even that. But we do not honour it enough in consistent regard to the lives and souls of our soldiers. How wantonly we have wasted their lives you have seen lately in the reports of their mortality by disease, which a little care and science might have prevented; but we regard their souls less than their lives, by keeping them in ignorance and idleness, and regarding them merely as instruments of battle. The argument brought forward for the maintenance of a standing army usually refers only to expediency in the case of unexpected war, whereas, one of the chief reasons for the maintenance of an army is the advantage of the military system as a method of education. The most fiery and headstrong, who are often also the most gifted and generous of your youths, have always a tendency both in the lower and upper classes to offer themselves for your soldiers: others, weak and unserviceable in a civil capacity, are tempted or entrapped into the army in a fortunate hour for them: out of this fiery or uncouth material, it is only a soldier's discipline which can bring the full value and power. Even at present, by mere force of order and authority, the army is the salvation of myriads; and men who, under other circumstances, would have sunk into lethargy or dissipation, are redeemed into noble life by a service which at once summons and directs their energies. How much more than this military education is capable of doing, you will find only when you make it education indeed. We have no excuse for leaving our private soldiers at their present level of ignorance and want of refinement, for we shall invariably find that, both among officers and men, the gentlest and best informed are the bravest; still less have we excuse for diminishing our army, either in the present state of political events, or, as I believe, in any other conjunction of them that for many a year will be possible in this world.

You may, perhaps, be surprised at my saying this; perhaps surprised at my implying that war itself can be right, or necessary, or noble at all. Nor do I speak of all war as necessary, nor of all war as noble. Both peace and war are noble or ignoble according to their kind and occasion. No man has a profounder sense of the horror and guilt of ignoble war than I have: I have personally seen its effects, upon nations, of unmitigated evil, on soul and body, with perhaps as much pity, and as much bitterness of indignation, as any of those whom you will hear continually declaiming in the cause of peace. But peace may be sought in two ways. One way is as Gideon sought it, when he built his altar in Ophrah, naming it, "God send peace," yet sought this peace that he loved, as he was ordered to seek it, and the peace was sent, in God's way:—"the country was in quietness forty years in the days of Gideon." And the other way of seeking peace is as Menahem sought it when he gave the King of Assyria a thousand talents of silver, that "his hand might be with him." That is, you may either win your peace, or buy it:—win it, by resistance to evil;—buy it, by compromise with evil. You may buy your peace, with silenced consciences;—you may buy it, with broken vows,—buy it, with lying words,—buy it, with base connivances,—buy it, with the blood of the slain, and the cry of the captive, and the silence of lost souls—over hemispheres of the earth, while you sit smiling at your serene hearths, lisping comfortable prayers evening and morning, and counting your pretty Protestant beads (which are flat, and of gold, instead of round, and of ebony, as the monks' ones were), and so mutter continually to yourselves, "Peace, peace," when there is No peace; but only captivity and death, for you, as well as for those you leave unsaved;—and yours darker than theirs.

I cannot utter to you what I would in this matter; we all see too dimly, as yet, what our great world-duties are, to allow any of us to try to outline their enlarging shadows. But think over what I have said, and as you return to your quiet homes to-night, reflect that their peace was not won for you by your own hands; but by theirs who long ago jeoparded their lives for you, their children; and remember that neither this inherited peace, nor any other, can be kept, but through the same jeopardy. No peace was ever won from Fate by subterfuge or agreement; no peace is ever in store for any of us, but that which we shall win by victory over shame or sin;—victory over the sin that oppresses, as well as over that which corrupts. For many a year to come, the sword of every righteous nation must be whetted to save or subdue; nor will it be by patience of others' suffering, but by the offering of your own, that you ever will draw nearer to the time when the great change shall pass upon the iron of the earth;—when men shall beat their swords into ploughshares, and their spears into pruning-hooks; neither shall they learn war any more.

APPENDICES.

APPENDIX I.
RIGHT AND WRONG.

Readers who are using my *Elements of Drawing* may be surprised by my saying here that Tintoret may lead them wrong; while in the *Elements* he is one of the six men named as being «always right.»

I bring the apparent inconsistency forward at the beginning of this Appendix, because the illustration of it will be farther useful in showing the real nature of the self-contradiction which is often alleged against me by careless readers.

It is not only possible, but a frequent condition of human action, to *do* right and *be* right—yet so as to mislead other people if they rashly imitate the thing done. For there are many rights which are not absolutely, but relatively right—right only for *that* person to do under those circumstances,—not for *this* person to do under other circumstances.

Thus it stands between Titian and Tintoret. Titian is always absolutely Right. You may imitate him with entire security that you are doing the best thing that can possibly be done for the purpose in hand. Tintoret is always relatively Right—relatively to his own aims and peculiar powers. But you must quite understand Tintoret before you can be sure what his aim was, and why he was then right in doing what would not be right always. If, however, you take the pains thus to understand him, he becomes entirely instructive and exemplary, just as Titian is; and therefore I have placed him among those are "always right," and you can only study him rightly with that reverence for him.

Then the artists who are named as "admitting question of right and wrong," are those who from some mischance of circumstance or short- coming in their education, do not always do right, even with relation to their own aims and powers.

Take for example the quality of imperfection in drawing form. There are many pictures of Tintoret in which the trees are drawn with a few curved flourishes of the brush instead of leaves. That is (absolutely) wrong. If you copied the tree as a model, you would be going very wrong indeed. But it is relatively, and for Tintoret's purposes, right. In the nature of the superficial work you will find there must have been a cause for it. Somebody perhaps wanted the picture in a hurry to fill a dark corner. Tintoret good-naturedly did all he could—painted the figures tolerably—had five minutes left only for the trees, when the servant came. "Let him wait another five minutes." And this is the best foliage we can do in the time. Entirely, admirably, unsurpassably right, under the conditions. Titian would not have worked under them, but Tintoret was kinder and humbler; yet he may lead you wrong if you don't understand him. Or, perhaps, another day, somebody came in while Tintoret was at work, who tormented Tintoret. An ignoble person! Titian would have been polite to him, and gone on steadily with his trees. Tintoret cannot stand the ignobleness; it is unendurably repulsive and discomfiting to him. "The Black Plague take him—and the trees, too! Shall such a fellow see me paint!" And the trees go all to pieces. This, in you, would be mere ill-breeding and ill-temper. In Tintoret it was one of the necessary conditions of his intense sensibility; had he been capable, then, of keeping his temper, he could never have done his greatest works. Let the trees go to pieces, by all means; it is quite right they should; he is always right.

But in a background of Gainsborough you would find the trees unjustifiably gone to pieces. The carelessness of form there is definitely purposed by him;—adopted as an advisable thing; and therefore it is both absolutely and relatively wrong;—it indicates his being imperfectly educated as a painter, and not having brought out all his powers. It may still happen that the man whose work thus partially erroneous is greater far, than others who have fewer faults.

Gainsborough's and Reynolds' wrongs are more charming than almost anybody else's right. Still, they occasionally *are* wrong—but the Venetians and Velasquez, [Footnote: At least after his style was formed; early pictures, like the Adoration of the Magi in our Gallery, are of little value.] never.

I ought, perhaps, to have added in that Manchester address (only one does not like to say things that shock people) some words of warning against painters likely to mislead the student. For indeed, though here and there something may be gained by looking at inferior men, there is always more to be gained by looking at the best; and there is not time, with all the looking of human life, to exhaust even one great painter's instruction. How then shall we dare to waste our sight and thoughts on inferior ones, even if we could do so, which we rarely can, without danger of being led astray? Nay, strictly speaking, what people call inferior painters are in general no painters. Artists are divided by an impassable gulf into the men who can paint, and who cannot. The men who can paint often fall short of what they should have done;—are repressed, or defeated, or otherwise rendered inferior one to another: still there is an everlasting barrier between them and the men who cannot paint—who can only in various popular ways pretend to paint. And if once you know the difference, there is always some good to be got by looking at a real painter— seldom anything but mischief to be got out of a false one; but do not suppose real painters are common. I do not speak of living men; but among those who labour no more, in this England of ours, since it first had a school, we have had only five real painters;—Reynolds, Gainsborough, Hogarth, Richard Wilson, and Turner.

The reader may, perhaps, think I have forgotten Wilkie. No. I once much overrated him as an expressional draughtsman, not having then studied the figure long enough to be able to detect superficial sentiment. But his colour I have never praised; it is entirely false and valueless. And it would tie unjust to English art if I did not here express my regret that the admiration of Constable, already harmful enough in England, is extending even into France. There was, perhaps, the making, in Constable, of a second or third-rate painter, if any careful discipline had developed in him the instincts which, though unparalleled for narrowness, were, as far as they went, true. But as it is, he is nothing more than an industrious and innocent amateur blundering his way to a superficial expression of one or two popular aspects of common nature.

And my readers may depend upon it, that all blame which I express in this sweeping way is trustworthy. I have often had to repent of over- praise of inferior men; and continually to repent of insufficient praise of great men; but of broad condemnation, never. For I do not speak it but after the most searching examination of the matter, and under stern sense of need for it: so that whenever the reader is entirely shocked by what I say, he may be assured every word is true.[Footnote: He must, however, be careful to distinguish blame— however strongly expressed, of some special fault or error in a true painter,—from these general statements of inferiority or worthlessness. Thus he will find me continually laughing at Wilson's tree-painting; not because Wilson could not paint, but because he had never looked at a tree.] It is just because it so much offends him, that it was necessary: and knowing that it must offend him, I should not have ventured to say it, without certainty of its truth. I say "certainty," for it is just as possible to be certain whether the drawing of a tree or a stone is true or false, as whether the drawing of a triangle is; and what I mean primarily by saying that a picture is in all respects worthless, is that it is in all respects False: which is not a matter of opinion at all, but a matter of ascertainable fact, such as I never assert till I have ascertained. And the thing so commonly said about my writings, that they are rather persuasive than just; and that though my "language" may be good, I am an unsafe guide in art criticism, is, like many other popular estimates in such matters, not merely untrue, but precisely the reverse of the truth; it is truth, like reflections in water, distorted much by the shaking receptive surface, and in every particular, upside down. For my "language," until within the last six or seven years, was loose, obscure, and more or less feeble; and still, though I have tried hard to mend it, the best I can do is inferior to much contemporary work. No description that I have ever given of anything is worth four lines of Tennyson; and in serious thought, my half-pages are generally only worth about as much as a single sentence either of his, or of Carlyle's. They are, I well trust, as true and necessary; but they are neither so concentrated nor so well put. But I am an entirely safe guide in art judgment: and that simply as the necessary result of my having given the labour of life to the determination of facts, rather than to the following of feelings or theories. Not, indeed, that my work is free from mistakes; it admits many, and always must admit many, from its scattered range; but, in the long run, it will be found to enter sternly and searchingly into the nature of what it deals with, and the kind of mistake it admits is never dangerous, consisting, usually, in pressing the truth too far. It is quite easy, for instance, to take an accidental irregularity in a piece of architecture, which less careful examination would never have detected at all, for an intentional irregularity; quite possible to misinterpret an obscure passage in a picture, which a less earnest observer would never have tried to interpret. But mistakes of this kind—honest, enthusiastic mistakes—are never harmful; because they are always made in a true direction,—falls forward on the road, not into the ditch beside it; and they are sure to be corrected by the next comer. But the blunt and dead mistakes made by too many other writers on art—the mistakes of sheer inattention, and want of sympathy—are mortal. The entire purpose of a great thinker may be difficult to fathom, and we may be over and over again more or less mistaken in guessing at his meaning; but the real, profound, nay, quite bottomless, and unredeemable mistake, is the fool's thought— that he had no meaning.

I do not refer, in saying this, to any of my statements respecting subjects which it has been my main work to study: as far as I am aware, I have never yet misinterpreted any picture of Turner's, though often remaining blind to the half of what he had intended: neither have I as yet found anything to correct in my statements respecting Venetian architecture; [Footnote: The subtle portions of the Byzantine Palaces, given in precise measurements in the second volume of the "Stones of Venice," were alleged by architects to be accidental irregularities. They will be found, by every one who will take the pains to examine them, most assuredly and indisputably intentional,—and not only so, but one of the principal subjects of the designer's care.] but in *casual references* to what has been quickly seen, it is impossible to guard wholly against error, without losing much valuable observation, true in ninety-nine cases out of a hundred, and harmless even when erroneous.

APPENDIX II.

REYNOLDS' DISAPPOINTMENT.

It is very fortunate that in the fragment of Mason's MSS., published lately by Mr. Cotton in his "Sir Joshua Reynolds' Notes," [Footnote: Smith, Soho Square, 1859.] record is preserved of Sir Joshua's feelings respecting the paintings in the window of New College, which might otherwise have been supposed to give his full sanction to this mode of painting on glass. Nothing can possibly be more curious, to my mind, than the great painter's expectations; or his having at all entertained the idea that the qualities of colour which are peculiar to opaque bodies could be obtained in a transparent medium; but so it is: and with the simplicity and humbleness of an entirely great man he hopes that Mr. Jervas on glass is to excel Sir Joshua on canvas. Happily, Mason tells us the result.

"With the copy Jervas made of this picture he was grievously disappointed. 'I had frequently,' he said to me, 'pleased myself by reflecting, after I had produced what I thought a brilliant effect of light and shadow on my canvas, how greatly that effect would be heightened by the transparency which the painting on glass would be sure to produce. It turned out quite the reverse.'"

APPENDIX III.

CLASSICAL ARCHITECTURE.

This passage in the lecture was illustrated by an enlargement of the woodcut, Fig. 1; but I did not choose to disfigure the middle of this book with it. It is copied from the 49th plate of the third edition of the *Encyclopćdia Britannica* (Edinburgh, 1797), and represents an English farmhouse arranged on classical principles. If the reader cares to consult the work itself, he will find in the same plate another composition of similar propriety, and dignified by the addition of a pediment, beneath the shadow of which "a private gentleman who has a small family may find conveniency."

APPENDIX IV.

SUBTLETY OF HAND.

I had intended in one or other of these lectures to have spoken at some length of the quality of refinement in Colour, but found the subject would lead me too far. A few words are, however, necessary in order to explain some expressions in the text.

"Refinement in colour" is indeed a tautological expression, for colour, in the true sense of the word, does not exist until it *is* refined. Dirt exists,—stains exist,—and pigments exist, easily enough in all places; and are laid on easily enough by all hands; but colour exists only where there is tenderness, and can be laid on only by a hand which has strong life in it. The law concerning colour is very strange, very noble, in some sense almost awful. In every given touch laid on canvas, if one grain of the colour is inoperative, and does not take its full part in producing the hue, the hue will be imperfect. The grain of colour which does not work is dead. It infects all about it with its death. It must be got quit of, or the touch is spoiled. We acknowledge this instinctively in our use of the phrases "dead colour," "killed colour," "foul colour." Those words are, in some sort, literally true. If more colour is put on than is necessary, a heavy touch when a light one would have been enough, the quantity of colour that was not wanted, and is overlaid by the rest, is as dead, and it pollutes the rest. There will be no good in the touch.

The art of painting, properly so called, consists in laying on the least possible colour that will produce the required result, and this measurement, in all the ultimate, that is to say, the principal, operations of colouring, is so delicate that not one human hand in a million has the required lightness. The final touch of any painter properly so named, of Correggio—Titian—Turner—or Reynolds— would be always quite invisible to any one watching the progress of the work, the films of hue being laid thinner than the depths of the grooves in mother-of-pearl. The work may be swift, apparently careless, nay, to the painter himself almost unconscious. Great painters are so organized that they do their best work without effort: but analyze the touches afterwards, and you will find the structure and depth of the colour laid mathematically demonstrable to be of literally infinite fineness, the last touches passing away at their edges by untraceable gradation. The very essence of a master's work may thus be removed by a picture- cleaner in ten minutes.

Observe, however, this thinness exists only in portions of the ultimate touches, for which the preparation may often have been made with solid colours, commonly, and literally, called "dead colouring," but even that is always subtle if a master lays it—subtle at least in drawing, if simple in hue; and farther, observe that the refinement of work consists not in laying absolutely *little* colour, but in always laying precisely the right quantity. To lay on little needs indeed the rare lightness of hand; but to lay much,—yet not one atom *too* much, and obtain subtlety, not by withholding strength, but by precision of pause,—that is the master›s final sign-manual—power, knowledge, and tenderness all united. A great deal of colour may often be wanted; perhaps quite a mass of it, such as shall project from the canvas; but the real painter lays this mass of its required thickness and shape with as much precision as if it were a bud of a flower which he had to touch into blossom; one of Turner's loaded fragments of white cloud is modelled and gradated in an instant, as if it alone were the subject of the picture, when the same quantity of colour, under another hand, would be a lifeless lump.

The following extract from a letter in the *Literary Gazette* of 13th November, 1858, which I was obliged to write to defend a questioned expression respecting Turner's subtlety of hand from a charge of hyperbole, contains some interesting and conclusive evidence on the point, though it refers to pencil and chalk drawing only:—

"I must ask you to allow me yet leave to reply to the objections you make to two statements in my catalogue, as those objections would otherwise diminish its usefulness. I have asserted that, in a given drawing (named as one of the chief in the series), Turner's pencil did not move over the thousandth of an inch without meaning; and you charge this expression with extravagant hyperbole. On the contrary, it is much within the truth, being merely a mathematically accurate description of fairly good execution in either drawing or engraving. It is only necessary to measure a piece of any ordinary good work to ascertain this. Take, for instance, Finden's engraving at the 180th page of Rogers' poems; in which the face of the figure, from the chin to the top of the brow, occupies just a quarter of an inch, and the space between the upper lip and chin as nearly as possible one-seventeenth of an inch. The whole mouth occupies one-third of this space, say one- fiftieth of an inch, and within that space both the lips and the much more difficult inner corner of the mouth are perfectly drawn and rounded, with quite successful and sufficiently subtle expression. Any artist will assure you that in order to draw a mouth as well as this, there must be more than twenty gradations of shade in the touches; that is to say, in this case, gradations changing, with meaning, within less than the thousandth of an inch.

"But this is mere child's play compared to the refinement of a first- rate mechanical work—much more of brush or pencil drawing by a master's hand. In order at once to furnish you with authoritative evidence on this point, I wrote to Mr. Kingsley, tutor of Sidney-Sussex College, a friend to whom I always have recourse when I want to be precisely right in any matter; for his great knowledge both of mathematics and of natural science is joined, not only with singular powers of delicate experimental manipulation, but with a keen sensitiveness to beauty in art. His answer, in its final statement respecting Turner's work, is amazing even to me, and will, I should think, be more so to your readers. Observe the successions of measured and tested refinement: here is No. 1:—

"'The finest mechanical work that I know, which is not optical, is that done by Nobert in the way of ruling lines. I have a series ruled by him on glass, giving actual scales from .000024 and .000016 of an inch, perfectly correct to these places of decimals, and he has executed others as fine as .000012, though I do not know how far he could repeat these last with accuracy.'

"This is No. 1 of precision. Mr. Kingsley proceeds to No. 2:—

"'But this is rude work compared to the accuracy necessary for the construction of the object-glass of a microscope such as Rosse turns out.'

"I am sorry to omit the explanation which follows of the ten lenses composing such a glass, 'each of which must be exact in radius and in surface, and all have their axes coincident:' but it would not be intelligible without the figure by which it is illustrated; so I pass to Mr. Kingsley's No. 3:—

"'I am tolerably familiar,' he proceeds, 'with the actual grinding and polishing of lenses and specula, and have produced by my own hand some by no means bad optical work, and I have copied no small amount of Turner's work, and *I still look with awe at the combined delicacy and precision of his hand*; IT BEATS OPTICAL WORK OUT OF SIGHT. In optical work, as in refined drawing, the hand goes beyond the eye, and one has to depend upon the feel; and when one has once learned what a delicate affair touch is, one gets a horror of all coarse work, and is ready to forgive any amount of feebleness, sooner than that boldness which is akin to impudence. In optics the distinction is easily seen when the work is put to trial; but here too, as in drawing, it requires an educated eye to tell the difference when the work is only moderately bad; but with "bold" work, nothing can be seen but distortion and fog: and I heartily wish the same result would follow the same kind of handling in drawing; but here, the boldness cheats the unlearned by looking like the precision of the true man. It is very strange how much better our ears are than our eyes in this country: if an ignorant man were to be "bold" with a violin, he would not get many admirers, though his boldness was far below that of ninety-nine out of a hundred drawings one sees.'

"The words which I have put in italics in the above extract are those which were surprising to me. I knew that Turner's was as refined as any optical work, but had no idea of its going beyond it. Mr. Kingsley's word 'awe' occurring just before, is, however, as I have often felt, precisely the right one. When once we begin at all to understand the handling of any truly great executor, such as that of any of the three great Venetians, of Correggio, or Turner, the awe of it is something greater than can be felt from the most stupendous natural scenery. For the creation of such a system as a high human intelligence, endowed with its ineffably perfect instruments of eye and hand, is a far more appalling manifestation of Infinite Power, than the making either of seas or mountains.

"After this testimony to the completion of Turner's work, I need not at length defend myself from the charge of hyperbole in the statement that, 'as far as I know, the galleries of Europe may be challenged to produce one sketch [footnote: A sketch, observe,—not a finished drawing. Sketches are only proper subjects of comparison with each other when they contain about the same quantity of work: the test of their merit is the quantity of truth told with a given number of touches. The assertion in the Catalogue which this letter was written to defend, was made respecting the sketch of Rome, No. 101.] that shall equal the chalk study No. 45, or the feeblest of the memoranda in the 71st and following frames;' which memoranda, however, it should have been observed, are stated at the 44th page to be in some respects 'the grandest work in grey that he did in his life.' For I believe that, as manipulators, none but the four men whom I have just named (the three Venetians and Correggio) were equal to Turner; and, as far as I know, none of those four ever put their full strength into sketches. But whether they did or not, my statement in the catalogue is limited by my own knowledge: and, as far as I can trust that knowledge, it is not an enthusiastic statement, but an entirely calm and considered one. It may be a mistake but it is not a hyperbole."